Troll Steps

Troll Steps

A novel by

Denver NeVaar

1st books - rev. 10/30/00

Table of Contents

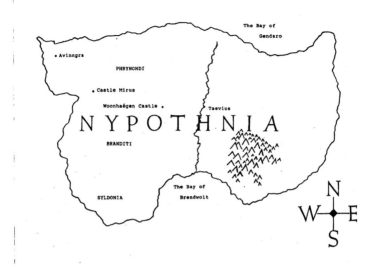

PROLOGUE

An Opening Excerpt

Fully in the beam of the morning sun stood a door, five times my height and equally wide. The painted windowpanes were bound in grey lead as smooth as a lady's hand-mirror. Such artistry seemed strange, or at least a jarring contrast to the rough, grey walls of the surrounding fortress.

I took hold of the door. It was hard to get a footing in the sandy soil. The oaken door began to budge, and with a tired creak of its ancient hinges, I stumbled past into a dimly lit passageway. My long gnarled fingers steadied me against damp, coarsely hewn walls while I strained my eyes at faint shadows just ahead. My oversized feet carried me deeper into the recesses of the fortress, tripping over cracks and crevices in the jagged limestone floor. Cool odors drifted into my nostrils and my ears wearied themselves to hear some small whisper of life. It was like walking through the previously undisturbed tomb of some ancient, forgotten ruler.

There! Faint strains of a lyre and someone singing. The labyrinth twisted to the left. Then I was falling, tumbling down, landing hard. I looked up at faces barely visible in the dim candlelight. I'd found the great wizard-king at last. From somewhere in the darkness came the question, "Who are You?" It echoed in my ears, as I groped within myself for a response.

CHAPTER 1

My Memories of the Carpenter, Brenwil;
the Baker, Relden; and the Alchemist

I'm just a traveller, collecting memories of people and places and times, not knowing my destination but somehow compelled to continue the quest; to come to terms with whom I've been and to seek out those who may help me escape my freakish and incomplete state. Like everyone else, there are things I like to remember and also things I struggle to forget.

I remember the carpenter.

Jostled to and fro, I fought to navigate the dirt path of ruts and rocks referred to as the Road to Avinngra. The narrow streets of a small city along the route compressed the mob around me, sucking us all in like so many rats into a snakes's belly. Surrounded by oblivious peasants, I felt safe, my form shrouded in heavy folds of deep-brown sackcloth, but I shuddered at the thought of entering a village exposed. The children generally stared at me with innocent curiosity.

The thundering of hooves and screams of wenches sent us scurrying out of the path of earls and squires on horseback. Racing toward the city gate, their only thoughts seemed to be of drunken revels waiting at a nearby pub. I'd never quite understood why the wealthy were wealthy because of God's blessing, as a bishop had said in a pompous speech in a town square through which I'd travelled. So many of the wealthy paid little heed to even the most basic of the church's teachings. Why then would God bless them any more than anyone else?

I stumbled against a rough stone wall and snagged my cloak on a jagged edge, but managed to maintain my cover. The wall was sparsely dressed with lifeless brown vines, as well as the shadow of a giant standing behind me. His iron grasp clamped down on my shoulder before I could run, and spun me about to face him. The pounding of my own heart fairly obscured his gentle question; I peered upward in amazement. His eyes had the strength one might see in a truly noble lord, yet his raiment was that of a poor peasant. The hand that held me fast was strong and gentle, though calloused and worn as well. To me, everyone seems tall, but I supposed he was slightly less than the average man's height, with exceptionally broad shoulders.

"You seem lost and perhaps in need," he said. "My name is Brenwil. Would you come to my house for some humble refreshment, little stranger?"

Befuddlement dulled my senses and stilled my tongue. He motioned me to follow and started off. My thoughts and feelings still jumbled, I hesitated, but began to follow. The door was calmly shut behind us a moment later.

I sized up Brenwil's small shop, the lowest level of some wealthier merchant's building. The floor of the shop was below ground level. One small window offered a limited view of feet moving by on the street outside. His hand touched my shoulder, inviting me to remove my cloak. At last I released the brown folds of fabric in my clenched fists. He slipped the ragged cloth from me, hung it on a peg by the door, and smiled. I shifted my weight from foot to foot and stared at the floor, wishing to hide either my abnormally large ears or my stubby limbs with hands proportioned for someone ten times my size. Yet I felt no coldness from Brenwil, but rather a reassuring warmth. He motioned and I moved to the table in the center of the room, where I found bread and water, a small carrot and an apple. He sat nearby, just watching, with that smile and those eyes.

As the light through the window grew scarce, Brenwil mused by the fire and I lay on fresh straw beneath warm blankets. A soothing chanting echoed in the streets, some friars going by, I guessed, and he opened the window a moment to see. With a more gracious smile than before, he thanked whomever it was and parted with a generous portion of bread. Then the chill of the night air was safely locked outside and I slept, dreaming of beautiful things I wished but didn't believe could ever be, at least not yet.

The rhythmic rustle of sand on wood rushed to my ears and the warm smell of broth filled the small cottage, as the dawn's light pierced the window. Brenwil smiled again, set aside the chair on which he was working, and took up a small rod of wood, a flute. A tune light and lively danced across the surfaces of the house to the table where breakfast was waiting for me. The simple meal was delicious, but my mind was preoccupied with the music as I went through the motions of eating. For a while the music made everything wonderful.

He stopped and handed me a rough block of some dark-colored wood and a small carving knife, then went back to the chair he'd been polishing. The block was slightly larger than a man's fist, each side about the same, but with lines running in many directions, swirling around knots and incongruities. The blade was sharp, but the wood was hard and the knots only made the task more difficult. I worked diligently, but the chips I carved away were very small and the overall shape changed with frustrating slowness. By the time the forest's coat had changed from green to hues of gold and scarlet several months later, I was able to present a crudely fashioned bird of glowing brown to my friend. Brenwil smiled. Then he took the bird and laid it on a shelf over the fireplace beneath a simple cross hanging there. It seemed a significant action, but I wasn't sure what it meant. He didn't often reveal his thoughts and emotions to me. He reminded me of a battle-weary veteran, someone who'd seen and felt much pain.

Crossing the room to an unevenly stitched case of sackcloth lying on a high shelf, he drew out a small flute fashioned from the same wood as my bird, simple in design but exquisitely beautiful. He gave it to me. My eyes were as wide as Brenwil's smile.

A village priest came in the next day on behalf of the local bishop, asking about having some statues carved. He hardly even noticed me at first. I sat polishing a chair leg in the far corner of the room, absorbed in my work. As he turned to leave I smiled in his direction and the priest suddenly jumped back, shouted something in Latin, then rushed for the door without looking back. Passing the window, the priest called from the street to cancel the order, saying that he'd find another carpenter. I tried to swallow while staring at a knothole in the floor. When I finally looked up, the carpenter was staring into the fire. Words of consolation died in my throat. With a deep and heavy sigh Brenwil turned away to a table he'd been sanding and continued with the work, looking up for one brief moment to force a smile in my direction. The rest of the morning was quiet.

An extravagantly dressed merchant burst into the shop late that afternoon, strutting about like a barnyard bantam, and I quickly slid under the bed. He'd heard the movement, however, and interrupted his introductory oration to call me out of hiding. His stare felt uncomfortable, but he finally shrugged and continued speaking with Brenwil. His request was a pair of candlesticks, to be ready two weeks hence if at all possible. Securing the contract, he turned with a flourish and barely gave me a parting glance as he strode out. The carpenter seemed relieved.

Thereafter I usually worked with my back toward the rest of the room when assisting Brenwil, and customers generally ignored me. That was certainly better than having sticks and rocks thrown in my direction, a frequent occurrence before my life in the carpenter's shop.

In between listening to merry melodies and Brenwil's wonderful stories, we'd pass the evenings sharpening my carpentry skills. However, one evening he became a little more serious, and began speaking of friends and relatives and happy times long past. Then he asked that I talk for a while, perhaps about the place from whence I came. I'd thought that the insatiable barbarism of my own land, which I'd left so long ago, would be impossible to forget; yet now my life there seemed so distant as to have been only a bad dream. What was there to say? There was too much. The lump in my throat forbade any answer at all. Brenwil smiled and my eyes grew wet.

"Perhaps some other time," he said. "Whenever you're ready."

As winter's coldness drew nearer, I was jolted awake one night by loud screams and wailing, angry shouts, and the smell of smoke. Brenwil ran to the window with a candle, then grabbed a staff and a cloak and hurried out. The door slammed shut behind him and I bolted to the window. Horses raced past and the smell of smoke was stronger. I ran to the door and peered out.

From one side of the village to the other, flames leapt from houses as from gargantuan candles. The dark horses bore riders with stringy black hair the length of a man's arm, who were clothed in ragged and dirty animal skins. Their familiarity made me feel cold. I saw children crying for parents and fleeing from the marauders, blood running in the streets, and the carpenter run through with a lance just outside his own door. Hot tears coursed my wrinkled face at the sight of such evil madness.

Nothing more than a shadow, with my ragged cloak locked between trembling fingers beneath my chin, I slipped through the streets. Beads of sweat stung my eyes, the pounding of my heart drowning out the screams of the dying and the wails of the mourning. I staggered into the shadows of the forest and wept, not even to be comforted by the song of my flute.

My flute had no song with which to comfort me. Brenwil had refrained from teaching me even a single tune. "Each must find the melody of his own heart," he'd said, "a melody that grows and changes with time." Often yet, I think I hear his soft, low voice, comforting and refreshing my weary spirit: "Find the melody, my friend. Yours is the only voice it can ever have."

I remember the baker.

The rats hissed and snarled before crawling resentfully away as I approached. The screaming hunger within me craved the moldy bread they'd discovered behind the bakery. A single bite made my stomach churn in revulsion, but I could find nothing more to eat. I closed my eyes against the wretched taste in my mouth, stumbled over some other bit of garbage, and nearly landed on my face. Someone caught me as I fell. But my stomach couldn't bear one second more, and I broke away and vomited the disgusting morsel I'd ingested. A hand came to rest on my shoulder and I turned and forced a weak smile to the man towering over me. He shook his head as he helped me up and took me into his kitchen.

A long table was covered with golden loaves, fresh from the oven, filling the room with the most enticing aroma I could imagine. I scrambled onto a high stool by the table and would have snatched a small loaf, but for the hand that caught my wrist.

"Patience. Patience, little one. I am Relden, the best baker in the land, and your hunger will be vanquished soon enough." He turned away again.

I again felt the tired ache in my shoulders and the weariness in my eyes and sighed. Only a moment later, however, a small cup of strong, spicy tea and a still-warm roll were set before me. Biting into that warm, buttery roll was sheer ecstasy. The baker laughed out loud at the amusing picture I presented and the obvious delight on my face. Then he went back to work.

Relden's ready wit and hearty laugh seemed to light the bakery with a brightness that made all burdens less wearisome. His hands were quick but gentle as he folded and twisted the dough into various shapes, picking it up and slapping it down onto the table's floured surface. He looked over at me occasionally with a whimsical smile and began to hum some tune unfamiliar to me. The rest of his shop extended forward to the street, the walls lined with shelves filled with all sorts of edible wonders. A man came in and cried out in alarm when he saw me; but the baker rebuked him, saying something about caring for the less fortunate. Is that what I was I wondered, less fortunate?

As the weeks passed, I learned the secrets of bread, the few ingredients mixed in the correct proportions so they'd work together. Too much or too little of any one thing and the rats in the alley would have an extra treat. When Relden began allowing me to mix the dough, perhaps a month later, I usually got it right. Once, however, I forgot the yeast and overdid the salt and came up with a round chunk of bread hard enough to be a cartwheel. I also had a hard time regulating the fire and baking time in order to achieve that perfect golden-brown loaf for which he was known and respected. However, each mistake was greeted with a chuckle and a sympathetic shake of the head, so I was encouraged to try again. He was pleased that my hands could knead such extraordinarily large quantities of dough so

6

well, my fingers reaching all the way around lumps even larger than those with which he himself worked.

Sometimes business was slow and instead of spending the evening preparing the next day's dough, we'd sit by the fire with the night safely locked outside. Relden's words meandered through memories of a wife and children, all gone due to pestilence and war, and questions about my past. But I never answered. I wished that I could've told him something, but the memories were still too painful. How could he have understood, when I myself didn't understand the strange people and places and events that had shaped and molded me into the person that I am? Who could understand my mother's silence and my father's noise? Who could understand the terrible cruelty of children and the abusiveness of the local priest? So I pressed these things into the recesses of my mind and concentrated on learning as much as I could.

Someone came into the shop one day wearing a strange cape. It was almost black but with metallic threads woven into it in unfamiliar patterns, like silver spiderwebs on the walls of a dark cave. His eyes were quick and sharp and set my nerves on edge. He reminded me of a razor, something which is somehow potentially lethal. He both intrigued and frightened me.

He'd received his bread and was about to leave, when he stopped abruptly, noticing my quizzical stare. A strange smile came over his face and I wiped the sweat from my palms a little too quickly. Then he left. Puzzled looks passed between Relden and myself.

The next day he was back. He seemed even more intense than before. He insisted that his bread come straight from the oven. Relden shrugged and headed for the back of the shop for the freshest loaf on hand, still cooling on a shelf there. My gaze followed, puzzled by this unusual exchange. Too late I heard the flurry of footsteps and the rustle of a large sack. Its stifling darkness enveloped me and some pungent odor melted my legs from under me. I think I remember being carried somewhere.

So it was that I met the alchemist.

Strange odors filled the gloomy air. My whole body ached from sleeping on the limestone bed I'd been given. The blurriness drained from my eyes and I saw the stranger hunched over a table covered with the most contorted and unusual equipment I'd ever seen. A small cloud of blue smoke rose from a shallow glass dish immediately in front of him and my curiosity drew me a step closer. He froze, then jerked his face toward me. He stared into the dark corner where I quickly sat down again and folded my knees up against my chest. Then he beckoned. I crept from my corner and peered over the table's edge to see various powders and liquids, some smoking or boiling vehemently. Then he touched my face, but something in his hands gave my skin a quivering chill. One of his fingers traced a fold of skin from my right eye to my chin, then stroked the other side slowly also. He knelt and peered deeply into my eyes as if to examine a treasure map inscribed there. I looked away, but his icy fingers forced my face back to his. Our noses almost touched and I squirmed to back away. He let go and moved away slowly, still staring into my eyes. His table held knives, wires, and oddly fashioned surgical implements and I imagined a cruel dismemberment on the altar of Science.

He handed me a bit of fresh bread instead, with a smidgeon of butter even, then motioned me to a low stool by the hearth. Within more optimistic moments, I couldn't be certain that he was truly evil and yet something about him was frightening. It wasn't his attitude, manner, clothing, or anything like that; it was something about his very essence. I took the bread and retreated slowly, not turning my back on him.

I watched him work and saw smiles, frowns, and expressions of severe puzzlement. Various colors, odors, and even sounds rose from in front of him and each time he would scrawl something into the book at his elbow. At last he rose, fastened the only door with some curious lock, and went to his own bed of coarse straw. There were no windows.

I stared at the fire wondering and questioning and wishing. Low, rhythmic snoring was the only sound for quite a while. I must've dozed off to its monotonous tones because it was suddenly dark. The fire had gone out. My eyes and ears strained

8

against the suffocating blackness and a rustling nearby nearly brought me to mindless panic. Then a spark touched a candle and his face reappeared across the room. My aching shoulders slumped with a sort of relief as he lit the fire to drive a damp chill out of the air. He reassured himself that I was still there, then took bits of powder from his table to paint various colors in the new flames he created on the hearth, each time turning to look for my approval. I nodded suspiciously.

His stocks of nourishment included mostly bread and cheese for the moment, washed down by a drink of some foul-tasting liquid he poured from a flask that hung on a nail near the door. I turned my attention to my ration of food and heard a faint creak as he crept out of the door and then tiptoed up some stairs. I was alone.

I swallowed hard and crept to the door. Quite strangely it was unlocked, but the end of the stairs disappeared into terrifying blackness. My fingers stole over rough stones and loose sand, guiding me higher into the dark shaft. When I'd gone quite a way up and rounded a corner, a single crack of light crossed my face and I scurried toward it, pressing the outer door with all my might, but to no avail. Somehow it had been secured on the outside. I heard voices but none were familiar.

I'd managed to retain my deep brown cloak and in desperation I wrapped it tightly around me and began to beat upon the door and shout as loudly as I was able. My hands grew numb and more than a couple splinters lodged in my fingers. A dog began to bark and growl viciously just outside. Still I pounded desperately.

Someone please let me out before he comes back, I thought desperately. The dog yelped suddenly and fled, as an angry voice called out and tore the door open to the blinding light of day. I stumbled and scrambled and ran in a mindless panic, upsetting some chickens and fruit carts in my flailing escape. Distantly, the alchemist cried out in alarm at the loss of his prize. I ran harder. I heard his rough voice rasping over the noise of the crowd, but only a few more feet and the town gates signalled freedom.

Why do I remember the alchemist? I suppose because I didn't think that I'd learned anything from him. I was too suspicious and frightened. He was too different from everyone I'd ever known. Yet he might've been able to help me more than many others. Perhaps someday our paths will cross again.

CHAPTER 2

Jonathon Ellick's Chapter

"My name is Jonathon Ellick," I said to the strange little person staring at me from the side of the road. "Tell me, if you will, why you keep yourself hidden within that brown cloak." Still there was no answer. "For goodness sake, do say something."

"You are a troubadour?" a soft but barely musical voice said at last.

"Why, yes, I am." I bowed quickly, removing my cap and swinging it widely to the side. "I bear news and recount stories wherever I go, but with all the tales contained within my head I still have no recollection of a person such as yourself." The little person shrugged, then looked downward almost apologetically.

"Have you lived in the woods long?" Realizing what I'd just said and remembering the person I was addressing, I quickly rephrased the question. "Or rather, have you ever lived within a community somewhere or other?"

"Once or twice I suppose."

"I imagine the woods must be a far more welcome place, free of others' judgements and possible rejections. I know I prefer the woods to the tangle of opinions that every town contains," I said. "I can hide from just about anything when I'm in the woods," I added.

"Have you ever hugged a tree?" I said, changing the subject. "Even when I can't reach all the way around, it makes me feel less alone when I do that. Trees are far easier to deal with than people. Trees always seem to hug me right back somehow. They have a slower sense of time and in many ways are much more simple and honest than people are."

"I like the way the woods smell," the little one said.

"Please forgive me for being so blunt," I asked, still wanting some sort of introduction. "Are you a boy or a girl? The way

11

your brown cloak covers everything except your face, it's not very obvious.

"What difference would it make?"

"Good question. I'm not really sure. But I would like to be your friend and it would help me to know what sort of consideration to show you."

"I'm something between a boy and a young man, I guess."

"You're not sure? I'd say you're a bit of puzzle, but then I always find puzzles to be quite intriguing."

"What was that song you were singing a moment ago, before you saw me?"

"Oh that's a popular one about a young lady locked in a tower, waiting to be rescued," I replied.

He smiled and I leaned down so that his gray-green eyes were even with my own blue ones. "Now will you tell me your name?" I put on my most welcoming and trustworthy smile while he stared back at me for a long moment. "Shall I give you a name?" I prompted. "Hmm. Let's see. Would it be Denalder, the conqueror of kingdoms long past?"

He chuckled loudly, apparently liking my little game.

"Perhaps Kretonin, with wisdom to spare? No? Well then, when the time is right you may advise me. For the moment it seems we are to be travelling companions." I snatched the edge of my short cape and danced away a couple steps, ending with a caricature of a professional dancer's twirl. "If you know any ballads, I'm always interested in expanding my repertoire."

A squirrel in search of sustenance rounded a tree just then, and screeched in alarm when it saw the little one. The smile on the wrinkled little face immediately faded. I heard a small sigh as he sat down on a tangle of vines just behind him.

"Oh, come now. Squirrels do that to everyone." I knelt and touched the small chin to turn his face up so we could look into each others' eyes again. "You seem to be a pleasant person," I said softly. "Don't let what you look like on the outside limit who you are on the inside."

He smiled again.

"Come," I said. "It's time to go." I stood up and repeated the skip and twirl of a moment earlier. "We travel while the sun shines, though the lady in the tower waits even longer because a dragon has taken her knight from this world to the next." I turned again for a moment and motioned enthusiastically for the little, brown, cloaked figure to follow.

Dusk had spread its misty cape through the forests and fields when we came to an inn called The Raven's Rest and entered, expecting nothing amiss. Only the innkeeper stood guard over the rough empty tables, polishing tin cups for the umpteenth time to chase away tarnish and dust. He barely glanced up as we entered.

"Prithee, noble keeper, a bit of ale or wine for my compatriot and myself, if you please," I said.

The keeper seemed not to have heard me. Something didn't feel right, but even the gloomy corners of the room were empty. Perhaps it was nothing.

Perhaps a tale would help. "Have you heard of the ruse of the Bregdillians, how they feigned defeat and entrapped the wicked knights of Trevatia within inescapable defeat, with the aid of an innkeeper such as yourself? The foolish knights had envisioned a victory party, never knowing the numbers of oppressed peoples hiding in the loft over their heads as they drank themselves into their final slumbers." Still, the keeper paid no mind. "The whole incident would've doubtless been forgotten were it not for the innkeeper's daughter who loved a particular young knight, and persuaded the mob to spare his life on the condition that she be sealed into a distant abandoned fortress with him for the rest of their lives together."

Long and low, I heard a pounding, a rumbling in the distance, but growing. Our host became strangely frantic and turned to the wall stacked high with ales of all kinds, brought forth glasses and mugs filled to the brim, and began rushing from table to table.

The door spun on its hinges and exploded against the wall, spewing dozens of thieves and rogues throughout the room, each boasting of some acquisition or exploit of the day. I leapt to the relative safety of the nearest dark corner, pulling my little companion along by a corner of his brown cloak.

"Maybe next time you'll remember how to shoot," a heavy man with a stubble beard said to a taller one behind him, slapping the second man across the chest with the back of his hand.

"At least I know what to do once I get my hands on it. The way you were hacking away with that dull knife of yours, there would have been nothing but mincemeat for the stew pot," the second man said as he wiped some more blood from his hands.

Half of a deer carcass, barely roasted, was flung onto a table near the door and greeted with knives and curses. The men ate like starved dogs.

With two huge mugs of ale already poured down, a highwayman with half of his teeth missing happened to spy us and bellowed over the din to a ragged-looking giant, who must have been the leader. This loathsome toad boisterously boomed a demand for entertainment from "the freaks in the corner."

I forced the biggest smile I could manage and leapt to the center of the room with a flourish.

"Oh the story's long been told, of the day they hunted the deer of gold," I began, accompanying each line with exaggerated gestures, "and pursued it long with heart and will, but lost it on the crest of a hill. As if into the light of the morning sun, it leapt up high and seemed 'twas gone. But turning round, its hooves were seen, escaping into the forest green."

At first the response was favorable, but my audience quickly grew restless. Someone bumped my leg and I glanced downward to see my travelling companion whirl his great brown cloak over their heads like the wings of a great owl, distracting their eyes and whipping the candle flames nearby to only a flicker. In the moment of gloom, I sprang through the nearest window, turning even as I landed to reach back inside for my small friend. Hopelessly outnumbered, I watched helplessly as he twirled the cloak around myself and rolled to the floor. The brutes who were nearest threw the table aside and scrambled drunkenly after him, to the amusement of those across the room. A few grabbed the edges of the cloak momentarily as he thrashed about against their ankles. I quickly looked for fist-sized stones on the ground beneath the window, something that I could throw to create distraction and hopefully successful escape. Nothing. I turned to the window again, contemplating a foolish rush back into the midst of the fray.

Stumbling against one another, the men were little more than a confused snarl of arms and legs on the floor. The giant leader seemed unconcerned and returned to slurping his ale noisily. Evidently the brawl in the corner was sufficient entertainment. Another table was flung aside and hit the floor with a startling thud. A little cloaked figure burst from under the mass of flailing bodies and tumbled toward the door, entangled in the brown material.

I raced around to the door, flinging it open just in time to allow the tangled cloth to roll past and to seize one corner of it. He landed in a breathless heap on the ground a couple paces away. I tried to smother a sudden laugh, remembering a couple acrobatic dwarves I'd seen perform last year in one of the arid cities to the south. I'd have to tell my friend about them sometime. His somber expression told me that he failed to see any humor in our situation, as he grabbed the cloak from my hand and strode off in silence.

"A most commendable escape, my friend," he said, trying to regain my composure as I hurried after him, putting distance between ourselves and those inside the building.

Gradually, small voices filled the night with harmonious lullabies. We rested on a carpet of soft needles beneath an old pine tree. I gave him a little hug, but didn't want to give the wrong impression so I immediately followed the hug with rolling onto my side with my back towards him and feigning sleep. The last thing I remember is the melancholy call of some night bird in the distance.

Then dawn's misty whispers rustled through the bushes, urging us on our way. His face and hands were bruised from the previous evening's incident, but thankfully no bones had been broken. We rose and found a path, this strange, little man and I, our destination unknown but still travelling companions for the present at least.

I revelled in our days together. He entertained crowds by pantomiming my artful words wherever we travelled. I wanted him to be truly happy, but could never seem to give him that. At least I could put a temporary end to his loneliness. If I couldn't give him a happy life, I'd at least try to give him one happy day at a time.

At last the piercing bite of autumn's end cut through our festivities and turned our trail southward to climates more balmy and soothing, where the icy blankets of the northern regions retreated from the sun's daily glow.

The people were a bit different here, more relaxed in general but easily agitated also. I'd been here before and even remembered a few names and familiar faces in the various crowds that gathered. But every crowd was different and telling the wrong story in the wrong place could mean running for our lives for a day or two.

I suppose what fascinated me throughout our travels together was the suspicion that the little one had experiences of certain extremes of life, to which I'd never even come close. Some have called me wise and some have called me foolish. I didn't have an answer so I just told other people's stories. In the little one, I sensed a much greater awareness and understanding than he ever admitted to having.

I caught him staring into the stillness of a stream that flowed slow and smooth under a bridge we crossed once, but he seemed embarrassed when he noticed me staring at him and hurried ahead while pulling his cloak up over his ears again. I almost asked what he was looking at, but reconsidered.

Another time as we left a particular town, a small child by the side of the road began to cry for some reason or other and he responded to the sound by increasing his pace. A while later we met a soldier escorting a funeral procession along the road and I quickly offered the explanation that my companion was from a much warmer climate, when asked why he was so completely covered by brown fabric. It sounded silly even to me, but the soldier didn't question us further.

It was a minor but daily challenge for me to maintain such company. I never heard anyone say that he was freak, a misfit, or an outcast, but their reactions were hard to misinterpret and hard to forget. Like the people we encountered in towns and along the road, I was under no oath of chivalry. Unlike them, however, I had no trouble seeing that there was something both mysterious and significant about this little person, qualities of character with which it was hard to avoid falling in love.

A few weeks had gone by and we'd just left a village by way of a dusty road. As we approached an intersection of several paths at the top of a ridge, a tall man with a haggard face approached us from another direction. There was an air of dignity and brutish power about him and something more that I couldn't quite define. Ah, yes, that's what it was, I realized.

"Hail, sir knight!" I called out. "Have you stories to share, tales of adventure or conquest? Where have you come, where are you going, and what have you learned in your travels?" The knight replied, more zealously than his posture foreshadowed.

"My name is Sir Trendall, my station having been granted by the great holiness, the celestial magistrate Sheznar the fourth, for whom I sought to raise a force of military might adequate to put an end to the nameless infidels, who oppress our land. Indeed I'm still intent upon that task and have little patience with those who run as rabbits whenever that danger appears." He paused for a moment, perhaps testing our lack of response in his mind. I nodded for him to continue, having no reason to question anything he'd said. "Even though you're clearly no soldiers, perhaps we could travel together a while anyway," he said. "It's been a long time since anyone has shared my evening campfire with me. The day is still young, however, and I must put more hills and valleys behind me before again lighting a fire and settling down for the night."

"As you've well said, I'm no soldier," I replied at last, "but merely a teller of tales, a singer of songs, and a bearer of news."

"If it's news you want," the knight interrupted, "then bear the news that Sheznar's forces will rise from the dust and reduce the barbarian hordes to the same before the wheat again ripens in the fields that surround us here. Given but a single chance, I'll wield my sword and lay to the ground the first three hundred that come against me, even if none stand with me against them."

"Oh noble sir," I said, laughing suddenly and causing Sir Trendall to stop and stare as if insulted. "Many's the tale I've both heard and told, but never one of a single knight prevailing against such odds. How is that you are so sure of your abilities? Surely your swordsmanship does not surpass that of the legendary founder of Avinngra, King Traenon," I teased.

"Who can say whether Traenon was actually that good," the knight said, "or whether he was simply facing a world completely untrained in such movements? Whatever Traenon was, I do know what I myself and my abilities are."

My little cloaked friend smiled and walked along just listening, later busying himself with maintaining a campfire, as the tales continued throughout the day and showed no signs of stopping even after we'd chosen a campsite for the night.

The smallest of the three of us was awake when my eyes finally opened the next morning, the sun just inching over the eastern horizon. The ashes were smoldering yet and I was able to coax a flame from them after a moment or two. Sir Trendall was still dead to the world, snoring on the ground where he slept. I suppose the word games we'd played long into the night might have seeemed childish to some. Perhaps they were, but no harm was done. Rather, I had added a number of new stories to my repetoire. For the moment, companionship held the three of us together in spite of whatever burdens, blindness, or blessings came with it.

Awakening suddenly and standing to go in a different direction than the way toward the south I'd suggested the night before, the crusader towered over the two of us as a tree over a low peasant's shack. Then he stooped momentarily to the little one's level and spoke in potent whispers.

"I know not why, but my soul rejoices in your company, most disfigured creature. Would you join my passage to a fair castle many days hence to live amidst the splendor there? I know also that his majesty there has knowledge of wonders unexplainable and may grant you aid, as to your form, if you wish."

This he hadn't mentioned the night before. As much as I wasn't in a hurry to travel alone again, if such a wizard-king existed then my little friend needed to seek him out.

"Sir Trendall seems very nice," the little one replied in my direction. "But we've only just met and you and I've been performing together for months."

"But isn't it worth a time apart, if this king of whom he speaks can correct whatever's wrong with you?" I argued. "I'm sure we'll see each other again someday. You know how much I get around."

"And what if there's nothing wrong with me?" He stopped suddenly, his eyes widening suddenly at what he'd just said. "I mean, nothing that he can fix?"

"Then nothing will have changed when we see each other again," I replied.

We spent the day in a nearby village and returned to our encampment just before dusk to plot the next day's departures. I insisted the little one go with Sir Trendall. If I allowed my little friend to stay with me in order to have a travelling companion and a fellow performer, it might be just the bit of selfishness that would keep him always a misfit and a freak in the eyes of others. He clearly wasn't happy with my decision on his behalf, though Sir Trendall seemed to be. The little one sighed and his shoulders sagged. Still, I had no intention of changing my mind. He shook his head as he turned back towards the evening campfire, drawing his brown cloak tightly around h is shoulders again.

"Then I suppose I'll be leaving with Sir Trendall in the morning," the little one mumbled.

Night drew its velvet wings around us and softly played the nocturnal symphonies of its woodland citizens. Then the small fire burned away and I slept fitfully until the cry of the wolf had faded as well and the warm glow of morning caressed my face. We rose, bid our fond farewells, and parted. I kept looking over my shoulder as we stumbled our separate ways, until forest and hill forbade us see each other anymore.

I would see him only one more time, and even that would be long after this. Then I wold never see him again. Years later, I would look for him but be unable to find him. Even in places we'd performed together, no one would remember him. Yet I

19

remember him; somewhat fondly, somewhat sadly. Mostly, I just wish him well, wherever he is.

CHAPTER 3

My Memories of the Knight, Sir Trendall; the Friar, Brother Benedict; and the Archer, Gairen

Memories hung heavily through the first few hours of that day's travels, as Sir Trendall and I plodded along. The air was hot and silent; neither wind nor bird song. The only sound was the dull trudging of our steps in the dust of the twisting road. Shadows shortened beneath our feet and at last he interrupted my moody quietness with a query concerning my origin.

I glanced up at him and smiled without saying a word; without wanting to say a word, still too preoccupied with thoughts of Jonathon and the wizard-king and the present journey. The knight seemed a stranger to me, though very kind in his own particular way. We walked on a good number of paces. Then, for whatever reason, I decided the time to tell my story had finally come.

"Far to the northeast where lies ice and snow in great measure through the months of Diandello, Euricia, Strychni, and Nehrvalden, is a city unknown to most but called by its inhabitants Taevius."

"Deep in a chasm of brittle sandstone, it survives by its hands and its teeth on whatever may fall prey, each generation multiplying the evils of the generation before. Dry weather brings choking dust. Wet weather brings sticky clay that clings like leeches wherever one walks or stumbles. Ice and snow may surround the chasm, but they never reach the bottom where Taevius lies."

My companion listened intently, and merely nodded for me to continue, when I paused.

"My father was towering and wavered between silence and storm. He'd sit by the fire at night with crude stone pipe, puffing smoke like the chimney and staring angrily at the orange-red flame-spirits as they danced, for hours at a time. When I woke he'd be gone and the wind would howl around the house like a

21

vengeful wolf with a taste for blood. The coarse grit in the dirt floor would bite my toes while my fingers clawed through nooks and crannies for something edible to put into my empty stomach."

"My mother sat in the corner, neither moving nor speaking. If she was truly alive at all, I was never aware of it. I only know that she was physically present. I never really knew my brothers and sisters. The younger inhabitants of Taevius ran in packs throughout the city and no one knew exactly to which family any of them belonged. They seemed to enjoy mimicking the battle stories told by warriors at council meetings, around the great fire in the central square of the city."

"All of this I saw, I understood, I felt deeply, and I remembered. I saw too, how the new snow on the high plateau was white and clean and pure, and how the wind's song was a dirge for these lonely people. I saw my own weaknesses loom over me like shadows I could never overcome. I saw the eagle, a bird of prey, but nevertheless beautiful in his strength to defy earth's restraints and break free to the expansive blue above. I saw rodents scurrying beneath the ground, surviving in spite of their harsh surroundings. I wanted to learn from them how such things were possible. But my father learned of my mental wanderings and beat me. It was wrong to dream, to seek beauty, to seek wisdom. None of these were part of his life and they weren't to be part of mine either. I should practice conquest instead. But I failed to conform, and felt his wrath again and again."

By this time, our shadows lay long on the road behind us. We travelled toward the rosy glow on the horizon and the silhouette of an ancient monastery etched itself into the skyline not far ahead. A tall, fair-haired friar who introduced himself as Brother Benedict greeted us warmly when we knocked on his rough-hewn door and requested refuge for the night. In moments, we were set to a table laden with warm broth and bread and joined by a handful of friars as merry as Jonathon Ellick had seemed to be. My troubles were momentarily forgotten as we supped and talked of all manner of adventures.

As the candles burned low, the friars moved off with their brown robes swaying rhythmically, but our fair-haired host lingered behind. The tapers were all but gone out when the attention of my two acquaintances turned to me and the reason for my journey.

"A burdensome blessing it must be," Brother Benedict began, "but I expect the difference of your form may be the gift of God that set you on this quest for your soul in the first place."

"A quest for my soul?"

"Yes," Trendall agreed. "It is the quest of every worthy person, though many who live never begin it. Others know not their own reflection until they're very old. It's a blessing for you to have begun while youth was still within your grasp."

"What could you possibly know of such things?" I responded to them both.

"Forgive me. It wasn't my intention to intrude," the friar said. "Many travellers have passed this way and they've all been my teachers. From each one I learned something more about those aspects of ourselves that are subtley revealed in each movement and wrinkle of our bodies."

"So what else does my unusual form reveal to you?" I asked, genuinely curious.

"It seems it's always the obvious that's invisible," Brother Benedict said. "What appears to me next is the place and people of your birth, a name not to be quickly spoken in crowded market squares. There are also indications of old wounds related to parental relationships."

"All fairly common things, wouldn't you also agree?" I said, a bit of skepticism showing.

"But what are the answers that you still seek? That's the real question." His blue eyes seemed to pierce the intellectual discussion all the way to the inner struggle I'd never confessed to anyone. I began to wonder if the friar and I had met before. Sir Trendall, exhausted, stumbled off to a bed somewhere. Brother Benedict and I, however, continued speaking a while longer. He brought a fresh candle and began again with his gentle probing questions, but my eyelids were so heavy that I don't remember what was said.

I woke to a sunbeam streaming in through a window at my elbow. Melodic tones echoed through the stone fortress with soothing reverberations and I found my travelling companion and the fair-haired friar waiting with breakfast. The friar laid his hand heavily on my shoulder and praised my understanding and wisdom, causing the knight to look up suspiciously, wondering what had transpired the night before. I wondered too.

We bid the friars farewell and continued our journey. The day seemed so beautiful and warm, as if everything on earth were smiling. Then the road wound into a wood, and the air became unusually quiet. Our conversation dwindled and soon the only sound was the quiet rustle of our shoes on the worn path. The day was nearly half gone when Sir Trendall sought to relieve the tension by urging me to continue my story.

Nervously I gathered my thoughts, but before a word could be uttered vagabonds and rogues exploded from the brush of the forest. The knight's sword felled the first few, but I had no weapon and they swarmed about us like angry bees.

The hissing song of an arrow suddenly pierced the heart of a foe. Others cried out as more arrows filled the air. The villains fled, and we turned to face our deliverer several paces down the road: a man, fairly a giant, obviously an archer of great skill. He approached slowly with strides of strength and confidence-- cautiously, but also without fear.

"Your aid is much appreciated," Sir Trendall said to the stranger. "Tell me from whence you've come lest you can bring us news of our destination."

"And what, noble sir, might your destination be?" the stranger replied, his great bow looped over his shoulder now.

"Castle Mirus," the knight replied.

The stranger's face clouded.

The knight searched the man's expression. "Upon your honor, sir, be open as the sky with us, for great is our hope to see the lord of that fortress for the welfare of my small companion."

The giant spoke more softly now. "My name is Gairen. When all was seen to be lost, I made my escape from there, from a battle fiercely fought for more days than we could remember. They seemed to come from everywhere, like locusts. They were dressed strangely in rough brown and black animal skins with swords the color of ochre. Their shields bore no insignia beyond the scars of ten thousand battles carved at every conceivable angle into the dull surface. So ruthless were these foes, so evil and so murderous, that a victory couldn't be foreseen. We fled with the king's own blessing, but where he's gone no one knows. The sure word is that he did escape with his wisest advisors and a number of good soldiers and servants, but neither does anyone know how nor where. The castle lies in ruins, but the great stone in the throne room lies unmoved and the handfull of suviving peasants look for his return." He paused. "What is it that ails your small friend?"

My travelling companion replied, but I didn't hear his answer. I leaned against a tree, sick at the news, recognizing the foe. My thoughts became a whirlwind and my vision blurred a moment. Gairen's strong hand against my chest snapped me to attention and my eyes jerked upward to his kind face.

A knot began to rise in my throat and I stammered out a protest. "Why must it be so impossible to run away? That which I'm unwilling to face won't evade my gaze and what seems long past continually reappears. Cursed is the one thus condemned while he yet lives." My thoughts thus spoken were obviously cryptic to them. I gritted my teeth through angry tears, swallowed hard, and tried to explain. "The blood of these foes is mine. Their language was mine. Their home was mine."

Silence hung in the air like an executioner's axe; the knight locked in awful realization, the archer not wanting to believe that my words were literally accurate. Stumbling to my feet, I asked the distance and found we were but a day's journey away. The marauders were close, much too close. I dared not endanger the lives of my companions any more than I unwittingly already had.

We walked without talking for a brief moment, though thoughts could've filled the air like so many buzzing flies around a stable in the heat of summer. Then, in the distance, came the sound of pounding hooves, hundreds of them, possibly thousands.

Gairen knew the woods well and quickly led us to a tree as round as a pregnant cow and hollowed by age. Climbing inside, he beckoned to the knight as the rumble increased, drowning the sound of our voices. Then the knight was inside also, but the evil hordes would be in sight in less than a second. I turned and fled, not wanting to reveal their hiding place and praying they understood.

The leader exploded over the hill on a horse dark as pitch. His eyes hit me like a hawk hunting a hare. His mount screamed and reared against the tight rein as his low, mocking laugh sent chills up my spine. It was my father.

CHAPTER 4

Sir Trendall's Chapter

The air grew still. The little one had fled and I would've abandoned our hiding place and gone after him, had not Gairen's massive arms held me fast.

"Sir Trendall, doesn't the code of every knight call for wisdom in addition to skill, and the ability to know when a postponed victory is more certain than an immediate one?" the archer whispered directly into my ear.

I sighed in agreement, knowing that we'd be little help against such a numberless mob. We were both torn by the thought of violence directed at one so small and so friendly. The traveller seemed to us to be a loving and noble person, but neither the archer nor I could discern the reason we believed so. What was it that, in the few moments since meeting him, had so knit our hearts to the misshapen creature?

The little one's cries of anguish cut to the core of my soul, but they grew fainter, gradually muffled by the pounding of hooves. In moments, the wood was once more silent, seemingly oblivious to what had just taken place.

"Either he's alive and I'll see him to safety," I said quietly when we'd climbed out of the hollow tree again, "or I'll kill the murderers with the same holy sword that labored against the unbelievers in the Land of Sacred Mysteries."

The archer clasped my hand and raised it between our somber faces in a wordless pact of allegiance to our little friend.

My thoughts were black as I surveyed the road by which our small comrade was taken. His brown cloak lay in the branches of a dead briar bush a pace or two from the road, and I retrieved the cloth as if it were a sacred object. We turned with quiet resolution and set out the way they'd gone.

Dark clouds rumbled overhead. The archer's eyebrows bent inward and he walked faster. I could barely match his great stride, but urgency flowed within each of us. There was a village just beyond this wood. Surely someone there would have a word to guide us. If only we could get some horses. How could we otherwise hope to catch up to the scoundrels before they reached their own country, assuming that was where they were headed.

Then the rain began to fall, muddying the path and obscuring the villains' trail. But then there lay before us a different trail to follow, one of blood. The village we sought was no more.

The pounding of rain on ruins of wood and stone and flesh was all that welcomed us. Nothing was untouched. We paced slowly through streets empty of movement but teeming with blood and debris. Bodies of men and animals alike lay beside the shattered forms of once-lively shops and houses. A few places were still smoldering, but the rain had extinguished the flames and thus prevented the devastation from being cremated and thereby hidden from all living eyes.

Scenes assailed my eyes that my mind refused to comprehend. We said not a word, as if we were walking through an evilly enchanted cemetery. Where the ruins of buildings stopped and the peasants fields began we paused, desperately searching the ground for signs to guide us in pursuit of these ravening wolves-on-horseback.

We continued on their trail, passing many more villages, each as desolate as the last; each corpse another voice crying out for justice to be done. We were no more merely two men against a thousand, but marched alongside an infantry of dishonored spirits. The forest and field seemed to understand and honored us with colors of scarlet and amber along our journey, but also warned that the icy bite of winter was creeping into the land. So much time had passed, perhaps several weeks, but nothing had been forgotten.

The frozen teeth of the wind and the mounting days without reaching our goal wore on our bodies and spirits. I was thoroughly trained in chivalry, to be loyal at all costs, to rescue those in trouble. Nevertheless, I found myself questioning whether the little one remained alive, whether I wasn't foolish to accept the hardships of this rescue attempt for one of so little worth in the eyes of the rest of the world's people, and whether in spite of our best efforts we weren't destined to fail against so great an enemy.

Night was falling around us when we glimpsed a small campfire through the trees ahead. We found a ragged old woman with a peculiar staff bathed in its meager light. She continued staring into the flames as we seated ourselves near the fires's warmth. Then she spoke, still without looking at us. "He's still alive, the one you seek, though he's in great pain. His pain is the pain of his people, who are clothed in self-hatred; not a pain that an apothecary might cure." She looked to me first, with a hollow stare, then to the archer, and then back to the flames. "They didn't see me as they rode by because I didn't want them to see me. The leader had a large sack tied to his saddle, containing your friend, I imagine." Again she looked up. "Don't concern yourself with who I am, how I know these things, or where I came from. These are irrelevant to you. You may call me Masra if you wish; but if no one remembers, don't speak of me. You may pass the night here; the fire will burn until dawn and then die away. I must journey on while the moon's light is available to me. I wish you good fortune in your quest. I suspect you'll see me again when the need arises."

She rose to her feet then and was gone before I could protest. Gairen's face veiled his thoughts and I couldn't think of a question to ask. We both lay down to sleep, our minds each in a peculiar muddle.

A faint wisp of smoke hung in the sunbeam that sliced through the morning mist to our campsite. This whole place seemed not entirely real, yet I could recall each moment that had transpired and each word that she'd spoken. The woman had left provisions by the stone upon which she'd been sitting and we had breakfast for the first time in days. Then it was time to continue onward.

The trail of devastation stopped after that. Villages were bustling with preparations for the long, hard winter ahead. We turned many heads, since travellers of any sort were unusual during this season. When I asked concerning a village named Taevius, all seemed puzzled and some called me mad.

The castle high on the ridge over a certain town seemed an obvious place for a knight to stop, but Gairen expressed hesitation. The banner flying from the tower was unfamiliar to me, but seemed somewhat similar in style to ones I fought for during Sheznar's great crusade. This particular one depicted a red tower on a field of blue. There was nothing especially unusual about the architecture of the castle nor about the fashioning of the guards armor, as they paced back and forth at the far end of the drawbridge.

We approached and asked to see the lord of the castle, introducing ourselves as emissaries of a great king in a distant land. The guards seemed wary of us, perhaps because of the archer's great size, but we were allowed to enter. A small page appeared and led the way. The castle's construction wasn't the finest I'd seen. The walls were sometimes crooked and many stones had been haphazardly placed.

The great hall wasn't particularly large and the man sitting at the far end of the table not impressively dressed. I assumed correctly, however, that he was the lord of the place. His manner seemed agitated and flighty, even fearful. He grew much more upset when the archer mentioned the wizard-king's name.

"Has Treston sent you? Does he know that you're here? Oh god, why do such things have to complicate my life so." His exclamations came quickly. The strange little lord began pacing about, wringing his hands and moaning in aggravation, oblivious to my blank stare. "All right. If I give you three horses and a month's provisions, will you leave me in peace?"

"That would be quite generous indeed and completely acceptable, I'm certain," I replied. "But why such concern? Has there been trouble in this region?"

He caught his breath a moment, but refused to answer.

"Well then," I said, "do you have any knowledge of a place called Taevius?"

At the mention of that name, his eyes nearly popped out of his head and his agitation increased a thousandfold. A more controlled advisor stepped forward and bid the lord retire to his chamber while his guests were attended to. The lord threw his hands up in the air, whispered agitatedly to the advisor, and marched out of the room shaking his head violently.

The advisor then introduced himself as the duke of Marhaéven and suggested we continue our discussion in the palace gardens while the provisions were gathered.

"I must first ask why you wish to know about Taevius." He was of medium height and a bit rotund, but appeared to be a thoroughly trained statesman. His hair was thin on top, but had evidently been a deep brown in his younger days. His eyes were kind, but suggested a somewhat wise and cunning nature where matters of administrative importance were concerned. A small sword hung at his waist and his manner was, in general, that of a confident but respectful leader.

"The tale is long but concerns a curious traveller we met on the road who was later kidnapped by some barbaric army, presumably from Taevius. Why he wasn't cruelly slain like so many others in the path of that horde, I know not; but we believe him to be alive yet and will rescue him from them if we're able. This traveller described himself as having been one of the invaders, until he fled the country of their origin. Now it seems they've found him and taken him back there. Does any of this make sense to you, or can you give us some insight that will encourage the success of such a rescue?"

The duke grew thoughtful and a silence hung in the air. Slowly he turned and wandered along a walkway through the garden. Then with surprising abruptness he turned and spoke quickly and barely above a whisper. "I will secure for you the provisions my lord has promised and a copy of an old map kept in our treasury, to guide you. Beyond this I can offer nothing except to tell that you've stumbled onto something very great and very complicated. One of the oldest of prophecies, one which has passed through a great many hands and minds, speaks of a person who may be your little friend. It would explain why such a great army would retrieve him. Come see me here when and if your rescue is successful and I shall explain more. For the moment, that's all I can tell you. Now go and god help you."

He pivoted on his heel then and shot through a door on the far side of the garden. I was left standing with my mouth open and my questions caught in my throat. The door slammed shut behind him and we stood where we were in utter astonishment.

The small page reappeared and led us to the courtyard where three horses were waiting, one loaded with the provisions. I mounted a dappled stallion, wondering if this whole adventure were some sort of joke or cruel game. Here was the map, rolled up within a long, thin bag which was tied to the front of the saddle. Loosening the drawstring at the top of the thin bag, I removed and unrolled the map, Gairen looking on. For a long moment we stared at the outline in silence. The larger shape was apparently the general shape of the land of Nypothnia, but through the very center from almost the very top to the very bottom of the landmass ran a jagged line that bore no explanation beyond a single point marked "Taevius."

"It's as if Nypothnia was nearly split in half," I heard the archer murmur.

"Perhaps in more ways than one," I answered, not quite recalling some strange old legend I'd heard years ago. "Wasn't there some ancient story about Nypothnia having been some sort of magical place, and that the end of that era was somehow connected with a tragic flaw in both the land and the people?"

Gairen shrugged, then climbed onto a large sorrel mare, taking the reins also of a charcoal-grey mare loaded with our supplies. A light drizzle began to fall as we rode out and heard the gates quickly bolted behind us.

The horses cantered along, oblivious to biting winds and sandy roads, for several days.

Before departing his company, the small page had identified the place as Woonhaégen Castle. On the map it was fairly centrally located, marking the journey as very long indeed. I wondered how the little one had traversed such a span to escape his people the first time. If the distance between Woonhaégen and Taevius was as great as the map suggested, the month's provisions would be barely enough.

Thankfully, this wasn't the case. Four days later, we were riding along at a good clip, when the horses suddenly began to shy and pull toward the left. My mount suddenly reared, and none too soon. There, not twenty paces ahead, a chasm

32

appeared, like a great crack in the expansive grasslands that surrounded us. I dismounted and crept to the edge of the abyss. Apparently I was on an overhanging ledge, since the opening was only ten paces wide; yet I could hardly see the bottom and the length seemed to stretch from horizon to horizon. It was the most mystifying land formation I'd ever seen.

"Shall I throw you a rope, in case the ground upon which you lie is unstable?" the archer called, when I'd explained the situation.

"No," I answered, "just go another ten paces away, drive my sword into the ground and tie the horses' reins to it. Then come and have a look yourself, but be careful to keep your distance from me. We don't want all of our weight in one place."

A thin layer of frost lay on the plateau but melted away several paces from the edge of the crevasse. The far wall of the chasm seemed devoid of vegetation and composed of ugly brown-grey sand and rock. A low whistle of surprise told me the archer had taken his first look into the chasm, somewhere to the right of me.

"So how do we get down?" I said.

"There's got to be a way somewhere, since that's where the murderers come from," the archer replied. The winds moaned strangely from below, as they careened up and down the narrow twisting gorge, and suddenly blew dust into my eyes. I squinted against the burning sensation and clawed my way back from the edge. I regained my sight and saw the archer rubbing his eyes as well. We turned toward the right, for no particular reason, to try to locate a way down. For a while we rode, then walked for a bit, then rode again, taking turns making brief forays to the edge of the chasm to look for anything below that might be helpful.

The sun grew hot on our backs. Then I heard a faint discordant sound. I dismounted and crept to the edge of the chasm once more and the sound grew louder. It was a confusing mixture of moaning winds, angry voices, and battle noises. The message of the queasiness within my stomach and the lump within my throat was quite clear: somewhere below was Taevius.

CHAPTER 5

My Continuing Memories: Returned to Taevius

I've found that each person is a combination of good and bad characteristics, qualities, and traits. In spite of whatever good or bad elements they possess, however, my friends are still my friends. At the moment, I missed them all terribly.

A month had passed since my father had reclaimed me as he would a piece of livestock, taking me from the lands to the west in a coarse woven sack strapped to his saddle horn, tearing me from faces and places I'd grown to know and love.

My reappearance in Taevius caused quite a stir, though none had noticed my sudden absence years before. For two weeks I'd seen only the blackness inside of that sack, smelled only the dry mustiness of its fibers, and heard only the pounding of hooves by day and the snoring and cursing of barbaric men by night. Dehydrated and weak from starvation, I was nevertheless still alive. When the world changes so suddenly and so completely and so drastically, memories become like dreams; it's a struggle to believe that they really happened at all. Then the sack was suddenly up-ended and I tumbled out onto the dusty central plaza of Taevius.

Jeering, angry faces encircled me. Towering over me, my father raised his arm and a vicious leather whip bit into my face. The mob cheered. The whip lashed out at me again. The mob cheered louder. I buried my face in my arms, lying on my chest in the dust. He kicked my side, flinging me over to face the whip again. The fresh welts on my face burned intensely and I began to cry. My tears seemed to infuriate him all the more. He began to shake and tremble with rage. Then he stopped, his arm raised, his whole body still trembling. He flung the whip from his hand and stormed away. The mob grew quiet and began to disperse. Someone stuffed me into the sack again.

My calloused skin thus bore a number of new scars when I was once again dumped from the sack onto the dusty earth in my father's house. He wasn't there at the time, so the unknown soldier chained me to the heaviest piece of furniture in the house. This was a large table in the center of the room, an oddly shaped slab of stone supported by some angular boulders half as tall as myself. The soldier hung his head, avoiding all eye contact with me until he was half-way to the door again. He turned and our eyes met for the briefest of moments. His eyes dipped toward the floor again and his mouth opened to speak but whatever words his mind had framed were never spoken. The door slammed and the noise of the wind outside was suddenly my only companion.

The shadows on the floor were long and dark when the dry creaking of the door's hinges jerked me awake. My father's face was wrapped in shadow also, but I sensed his burning stare. Then some strange dead bird was flung at me to be prepared for his evening meal.

My fingers trembled as I began to pluck the feathers from the bird, glancing to the towering figure still standing in the doorway. A loud thud told me I was alone again. The dim light from the fire on the hearth gleamed iridescently on the wings of the bird in my hands and I mourned its sightless eyes and stilled tongue. What sort of song had this creature been able to sing?

My father returned a while later and snatched the bird from the edge of the hearth for inspection. From the angry manner in which he began to work on the bird himself, I knew that I hadn't done as well as he'd expected me to.

There is some unexplainable bond between parent and child that can never be broken. It may be argued that I obeyed my father only for reasons of physical survival, but I know that it was more than that. I really did want to please him. Perhaps if I could just be good enough, he'd become the loving father I'd always longed for him to be.

He shook the bird at me when he finally found it to be satisfactorily prepared for roasting. "You're more worthless than an arrow-shaft filled with worms. I've done no evil severe enough to deserve a son such as you."

My hands trembled slightly as I felt waves of hatred and anger wash over me. I studied the floor, the wrinkles in my

36

hands, the fibers in my clothes. When I looked up again, my father was preoccupied with building up the fire to roast his supper and drive out a chill which was creeping into the house. I watched as he tore apart the bird a while later, tossing each small bone to me when it no longer held enough meat to interest him.

Unofficially, I'd been made a universal scapegoat; though, in retrospect, that may have worked in my favor. When I was suddenly considered the cause of every evil and a living bad luck charm, no one wanted me around. Everyone avoided me. The jeering stopped. No one threw rocks at me anymore. The days were long and lonely, but they were also quiet and in some sense peaceful because no one ever stayed in the house with me except to sleep and to eat. Even my mother in her seemingly catatonic condition would wander out each morning, though I never knew where she went or what she did. Very little had changed since my childhood, years before.

My father had intended to use me to make himself appear a hero, but he was rapidly becoming the town fool. Evidently, when I'd escaped years before, it had somehow disgraced him. His reclamation and public punishment of me were supposed to have redeemed his soiled reputation as a warrior. When the rest of those living in Taevius began to see me as a liability, they began to shun him also.

In forgetting the horrors that comprised daily life in Taevius, I'd also forgotten some of the language. I quickly recalled enough to understand much of what was said around me, but was never able to respond. One morning the door was flung open and the room quickly filled with children of various ages. A man I hadn't seen before entered and began lecturing to them while gesturing at me. He used a lot of big words that I couldn't remember.

I peered around at the sullen faces, wondering which ones might be my brothers and sisters; then wondering if they even knew the meaning of such words as "brother" and "sister." I was so strange to them. Their bodies were more typically proportioned and my deformities mystified them. Some of them hadn't even been born when I'd first escaped. I stumbled through my own native language, trying to tell them of the beautiful things in other lands, but to them it was all simply treasure to be plundered. I fell silent before their empty stares. I began to wonder whether I was insane to believe such far-away things really existed as I remembered them. Had all those happy times been nothing but dreams and wild imaginings? Were they truly memories? The greed and violence that saturated all of life here weighed heavily upon my spirit and I began to lose hope, to wonder if my freedom had also been only a dream. I needed to escape again and it needed to be soon.

CHAPTER 6

Gairen's Chapter

We'd reached the chasm, yet there was no apparent path downward. It was as if the earth had cracked open and allowed a bit of sunshine to touch a subterranean hell. The sides of the chasm were relatively smooth near the top, which was about all we could clearly see for the moment, with a few caves scattered here and there. The stone which comprised this topographical anomaly looked to be extremely unstable. I began to wonder why the entirety of Taevius hadn't long ago been buried in an avalanche.

"Gairen," Sir Trendall called to me. "Take this spare lance of mine and drive it deep into the ground to serve as a tethering post for the horses, since there's not a single tree or bush anywhere within sight."

It took an hour or so of searching but I finally found a place from which to begin our descent. The air was cold, but dry. We began creeping downward, one fingerhold at a time. Unpredictable gusts of wind began tearing at our clothes when we were perhaps a dozen times my height below the rim of the canyon. Its vicious moaning didn't serve to build either our confidence or our concentration.

The succession of fingerholds gradually became a path, which wound from one overhang to another, each switchback cutting underneath the last such that the chasm grew ever wider. Several hours into our trek, we came upon a broad ledge at the mouth of a cave, with evidence of cooking fires and temporary occupation by unknown persons. A few charred logs were clumped against one side of the cave's entrance, with bits of broken pottery and crude stone tools nearby. A small rag of red-brown fabric flapped in the wind where it had been impaled on some sort of stake a few paces from the former cooking fire. It didn't look like anyone had been there in quite some time.

39

Then I peered into the darkness of the cave itself, entered a few steps, and waited for my eyes to adjust to the gloom. Skeletons. Dozens of human skeletons.

"Is this the way they bury their dead?" I muttered.

"Or is it the fate of their captives?" Sir Trendall responded, glancing to the now-cold cooking fires again.

The bones were all heaped together, but more than a few skulls were easily visible. "Who are these people of Taevius?" I whispered, staring at the mass of bones.

We continued downward. The sounds of Taevius had been growing louder and dim outlines of stone and mud structures began to be visible below us. The path grew slowly wider and began to slope outward. We were more than halfway down. The chasm apparently had been a tunnel of some sort, formed by an underground river aeons ago, the top surface having finally eroded more recently to allow an opening into the space. The boulders along the path grew larger as well, evidently left over from minor avalanches long past, providing welcome screening from those wandering the streets of Taevius below who might cast a glance in our direction. Strangely, it seemed warmer here than it had at the top.

We arrived just before dusk at a ledge just some twenty paces above the edge of the city, which seemed to extend infinitely in both directions on the narrow chasm floor. The homogeneity of the city made a haunting picture: squarish mud and stone structures easily numbering in the thousands, all roughly the same size and shape, with dark wooden doors and no windows. Each also had an irregularly shaped hole in the roof, through which emerged a faint whisp of smoke. Except for the dark wooden doors, everything seemed to be the same shade of brown-grey: the houses, the streets, and the walls of the chasm. Even the people all looked the same: long, stringy, black hair, clothing made from ragged and dirty animal skins, and short but gaunt-looking faces. Taevius: no color, no variety, and apparently no happiness.

The streets were anything but quiet. Soldiers and wenches strode angrily from one building to another, carrying crudely shaped cups or bottles, seemingly bitter about everything. The young ran like wild dogs through the streets, violently attacking any who dared show fear or weakness. The whole place seemed devoid of beauty.

Dusk passed into twilight as we stared at the street life below. Sir Trendall nudged my elbow, and pointed a little higher and to the right. I stared. On a ledge on the far side of the chasm, illuminated by the light of the moon now inching its way into the narrow, indigo-hued strip of sky high above us, grew a single flower as white as snow and as simple as the hermits of Hernondia; quiet and beautiful and alive.

The streets grew quiet at last, except for a few angry shouts here and there. The young bullies finally split up, after a peculiar parting ritual of striking each other violently across the jaw. After another hour of undisturbed waiting, I crept from our hiding place and led the way down.

At the first small building we came to, we heard only loud snoring. The next was likewise, as was the next and the next, until we wondered if we'd ever find the little one in this maze. We searched all night. We were crossing a central plaza in the city just before dawn when Trendall stopped and gazed around as if contemplating something.

A frown of concentration abruptly faded from his face as he knelt and began carving something into the ground, using a small dagger that had been hanging from his belt. I stepped closer to see and gave the knight a smile and a nod, recognizing the unusual greeting.

We slipped back to our ledge quietly, interrupted only once along the way. A soldier stumbled out of a door along our path. When a rasping female voice called to him, however, he sneered and frowned, then re-entered and slammed the door.

We chose an unstable sandstone cave near the our previous ledge and settled in to wait and watch whatever would happen below. My gaze passed uncertainly to Sir Trendall and he returned it. Waiting, listening, hoping, praying--if all went well, the little traveller's deliverance was near.

CHAPTER 7

My Continuing Memories:
Imprisonment in Taevius

There seemed to be no way to escape. If only my friends were here, perhaps they could think of something but then again, what could they do against so many? It seemed I was on my own, as before.

I'd always been on my own in some way or other. In Taevius, the general appearance was that all were part of a massive, pseudo-military force, but here and everywhere else the reality remains that people are individuals and each is unique in some way. At the very least, there's a quality of separateness to each life. Birth, growth, and death are always faced alone, no matter how many others are present.

I'd studied the lines in the sandstone table, wondering if there was a crack in the stone that I could exploit. I'd also studied the shape of the chains binding me, hoping to find the proverbial "weak link." Both were now indelibly etched into my memory. The table was a slab of stone as thick as a handbreadth, the top surface being somewhat oval in shape, resting on four irregularly shaped boulders. The chains binding my hands and feet encircled one of these boulders, so my first task would be to either break links of chain as thick as my fingers or else to move a stone so heavy that a dozen men had been required to assemble the table when the dwelling was first assembled.

In most houses in Taevius, the table was the only piece of furniture. People slept on piles of straw along the walls and sat on the floor when they grew tired of standing. A few had placed additional boulders within their houses, upon which to sit, but that was viewed by most as a luxury that would make a warrior weak. Most of daily life was conducted in outdoor public areas and consisted primarily of preparing in some way for the next year's season of plundering.

I didn't know where to begin. For a moment I thought of the unknown soldier who'd almost spoken to me that first day, the one who'd chained me to the table. I wondered what he'd wanted to say. If in spite of all odds, I could be born and grow up within Taevius, then possibly there were others like me also, just doing their best to quietly survive.

I discovered one morning that each of the links within my chains sounded a slightly different note when tapped with a small loose stone I'd found near the hearth. Before long I was composing simple melodies, but of course only when my father was away. It was a kind of music, but I couldn't decide whether the sounds more closely resembled muffled bells or tiny cries of pain. Still, it was a kind of music. My mother heard it once. She stopped, listened, and for the first time turned to look into my eyes. I sensed a great emotion, but no words were spoken. Her blank expression almost gave way to a faint smile.

My father had the key to my chains tied to the hilt of his dagger, which he carried with him always. I hadn't yet had an opportunity to steal the key. I tried telling myself daily that nothing was impossible, but the words sounded more hollow each time I said them. As if wrestling with an intangible, constricting briar coiled around my heart and lungs, I clung to a nameless, faceless hope which would change everything.

One morning a sudden gust of wind opened the door just enough for a little brown sparrow to alight and peer inside. He began chirping out a tune so vigorously, I would've thought he'd just come from Brother Benedict's friary. I'd never seen a sparrow in Taevius before. My father still slept soundly so I embraced the moment of beauty with a smile, the first one since my return to Taevius.

An explosion on the side of my head sent me sprawling. A thrown heavy boot banged against the door, but didn't drive it completely shut. My father wasn't so soundly asleep as I'd thought. I turned my aching head to see him towering over me, his hand raised to strike again. I glanced to where the sparrow had been and was thankful the bird had escaped.

"If you ever disgrace my house with such weakness again, you'll live to regret it! Not even death will be your refuge, you

44

disgusting little maggot! You haven't begun to experience how unpleasant life can be!"

I turned my throbbing head to look at him, but the light from the doorway cast shadows across his eyes and I saw nothing but the iron set of his jaw. I trembled in spite of myself, thus incurring another blow before he stomped to the fireplace to light his pipe and slurp down some broth. A trickle of blood and a trickle of water slowly raced down my face, arriving at my chin together, and I buried my face in my arms on the dusty floor.

Suddenly, shouts began to echo in the street. Someone pounded violently on the door and flung it open without waiting, to demand my father's presence at the arena where war council meetings were held. My father's expression instantly changed from anger to something akin to fear. He left his pipe on a ledge over the fireplace, as he and the other rushed out, slamming the door loudly behind them.

I was puzzled. Nothing unusual ever happened in Taevius. It was too far from everywhere else.

Moments later the door flew open so fast that it slammed against the wall, leaving my father's angry silhouette in the doorway. "Someone's written words of friendship in the council place of war. They've carved words of weakness into our place of strength. It's a severe offense, a disgracing of all that is sacred to us!"

No answer could deflect my father's angry fist. The first blows drove pain throughout my body. The later ones drove a pounding thud into my ears. The last ones I don't remember. I do remember somehow knowing that I was no longer alone.

CHAPTER 8

King Wolten's Chapter

"Namaste, little friend." I read the words within my mind rather than pronouncing them for anyone else to hear. I had believed that no one else in Taevius knew the old languages of Avinngra and other foreign places.

"What is the meaning, King Wolten?" The soldier standing to my left had a very frightened look on his face.

"It means that the return of the misshapen boy has drawn other unwelcome people to our city as well," I said. "It means that they have no respect for our ways and especially not for our religion. Go and bring the father of the misshapen one here at once."

The soldier was off at once, as fast as he could run. I tried to hide my confusion from the gathering crowd in the few moments before he returned. Why would anyone come all this way to rescue a freak? Rescue. I couldn't think of any other reason anyone would approach a hornet's nest like Taevius. "Namaste." A particularly old religious greeting reflective of a ridiculous belief that some sort of divine light existed within all things. "Little friend." No one was anyone's friend in Taevius. It's part of what made governing such a violent population possible.

This was supposed to have been just another day in Taevius, but a frantic banging on the gong in the central plaza of the city prevented me and everyone else from finishing even the first meal in the routine sort of way. Faced with a mob becoming ever more fearful of an attack by outsiders, I needed to think quickly. There obviously wasn't time to sneak away to the secret library cave, the very existence of which was unknown to everyone in Taevius except my immediate family.

The Council of Nine was almost entirely present and the father of the misshapen one would also be here in another few moments. With a sigh I moved to the center of the plaza and waited for the council members to form the usual circle with me, the rest of the people forming a circular mob around us a couple paces away on all sides, as we always did when there were important decisions to be made.

This time, however, each member of the council simply stared at me, none of them being able to read the inscription carved into the ground between us and thus not knowing whether it was an innovative prank or a significant threat. Apparently, the outcome of the incident rested entirely with me.

"There is no danger," I said. "No enemy would have betrayed their presence if they meant to attack. Whoever has done this has something else in mind, a manipulation of some sort. Our ways of dealing with such things in the past have served us well and will serve us well again."

"Here comes Trokon," a council member to my right said, pointing behind and beyond my left shoulder.

I turned to see the high priest approaching, the crowd parting to let him pass, keeping their distance from the strange, angry man. He even wore his ceremonial seven-horned crown that identified him as supreme spiritual leader, with dried and fraying snakeskins trailing from the sides of the headpiece.

"This is purely a political situation," I called to him before he'd completely reached the inner circle.

"The plaza of war has been defiled and must be cleansed," he snapped back at me. "The people must see rituals of protection performed, in order to put an end to their fears."

"Then when the council has finished its discussions, you are free to do all of the rituals you wish." A hot stare passed back and forth between us, testing who's authority would stand. Tensely exhaling, he stepped backwards to become an eleventh person in the inner circle.

A commotion on the edge of the crowd beyond our small circle alerted me to the return of the soldier with the misshapen one's father. I gestured to two of the council members to open our inner circle slightly, as the father was brought to us, the messenger soldier standing two or three steps behind him to prevent any escape.

48

"What is your name?" I said, drilling into him as hard as I could with a cold stare.

"Bewelden, my king, but please, I haven't been out of my house since last night and have no knowledge of whatever has happened, that you'd need to speak with me this way," he stammered.

I pointed to the ground. He looked down at the writing, but couldn't possibly have known what it said, so he looked at me again. "Trokon has correctly identified it as a defilement. I," turning to stare calmly at Trokon, "have correctly identified it as no serious threat to the welfare of our city." Turning back to Bewelden, I continued. "You can see for yourself what a disturbance it has nevertheless caused, though I'm quite certain that none of this would've happened if you'd had the good sense to kill the wretched child when it was born. Perhaps you could still accomplish that and deliver all of us from such irritations in the future." Again I drilled a cold stare into him as hard as I could, maintaining a reasonably blank expression.

Bewelden's mouth hung open, his tongue moved to say something, but no words came out. Then he broke through the circle and fought his way through the crowd, everyone's eyes following him as he ran back to his house. Distantly I heard the door slammed open, the thud of a club against flesh and bone, and some faint cries of pain.

Moving with the crowd toward the house, people around me began to cheer. By the time I'd almost reached the place, the cries were subsiding into probable unconsciousness. Perhaps this would be the end of the problems that this small freak brought to us. I had no desire to look at him again, however, even to see whether he was dead or not, and stopped about twenty paces from the house.

A greater concern to me, which everyone else had thankfully forgotten, was the probability that someone else was here, one or perhaps more who were clearly not Taevian.

Back at the central plaza, Trokon was just finishing his ritual of supposed cleansing. I glared at him, but he didn't seem to notice, occupied as he was with covering the inscribed words with different colors of sand and spit.

Closing my eyes for only a second or two, so as not to attract attention or betray unusual abilities, I psychically scanned the city and the surrounding walls of the chasm for any anomalies. In the timeless realm of spirit, however, the caves and homes had held far too many different creatures to discern anything unique within the day at hand. I opened my eyes and scanned the walls visually, but still saw nothing. Yet something mysterious in the back of my head told me someone was there, somewhere, hiding and waiting. Waiting for what? I could only guess, but all of my guesses were far less encouraging than the words I'd spoken to the people.

Returning to my own larger administrative house, I summoned my personal guards. "If any of you ever breathe a word of this, I will personally slit your throats and leave you to choke to death on your own blood," I said. "Knowing, however, that you will never make me fulfill that threat, I tell you now that someone from outside of Taevius is here but not with sufficient forces to simply attack. Under no circumstances are you to say anything to anyone, nor do I want you investigating the caves on either side of the chasm. I don't need this nameless, faceless enemy overcoming you one man at a time. I do want you to patrol the streets in pairs, however, and keep your eyes on the caves and the boulders beyond the last houses on each side. If you see anything at all, one of the pair will stay and watch and the other will come and find me immediately. I'll be walking throughout the city as well, doing the same sort of hunting for this unknown intruder. Any questions?" None of the dozen frightened faces peering back at me moved. "Then go." In seconds I was alone again.

Hours passed, each one increasing the tension within my mind, as no new clues to the mysterious one or more intruders was found. I returned to a perch on the roof of my house just as the chasm began to glow orange high above, signalling the approaching night. Doubtless something was about to happen, but who could say what. I stared toward Bewelden's house, knowing the next intrusion would be there.

A larger shifting shadow near the house caught my eye and I jumped to my feet. No, perhaps it was nothing. Not likely, but

50

perhaps. I stared. Then a man leapt to the roof of that house, much taller and broader than any Taevian soldier I'd ever seen, with a bow as long as I was tall. A single arrow shot from his fingers toward a cave high and to the right from where he stood, a place somewhat between he and me. A faint crumbling noise a second later told me what was in store, something far worse than any of my wild guesses.

Scrambling down to the street level, the rumble of tumbling rocks and boulders rapidly increased. There wasn't even time to sound an alarm, but everyone seemed aware of what was happening anyway. Pandemonium was what was happening, the air filling with dust and sand. A more perfect diversion couldn't have been devised. The victory was clearly theirs and there hadn't even been a battle.

The dust and screams seemed irrelevant now. So this was how Taevius would perhaps finally be ended, centuries of hatred, violence, and revenge buried at last. Perhaps it was best.

I stepped through a cloud of dust to see the giant and another man with a long sword coming out of Bewelden's house with the small misshapen boy in the giant's arms. I shook my head slowly, removed my crown of horn, snakeskin, and animal bones and threw it to the second man. I would start all over again when the dust settled, building a new Taevius even as my ancestor Brenwoldt had built the first one.

The second man caught the crown on the point of his sword, however, and threw it back to me. "I have come here to rescue a friend, not to defeat a people," he said. Then he turned and ran after the giant. Moving to a more central street where I'd be safe from the avalanche, I watched as they scrambled back up a particular trail, finally disappearing in the mix of shadow and dust and reverberation that filled the chasm.

When the avalanche had finally spent itself and over half of the city lay in ruins, I looked around at the ragged world, which was mine to rule if I could. A sliver of moon light from high above began to creep down the far wall in the deepening gloom and a certain bright spot caught my eye. A flower, perhaps a moon flower, so named because of exactly what I saw. My grandmother had said there were occasional quiet whispers of a

51

time when such flowers had filled the chasm, but that Brendwolt had worked hard to erradicate them because they were at odds with his own militaristic agenda. It seems he hadn't completely succeeded.

How quiet the night seemed now, how rich the colors of stone and sky and moon and stars. Ah well, what of it. In the morning, the Taevian army would rise again. Already, hundreds of people were climbing over rocks and debris, reclaiming weapons, clothing, and food supplies from the cataclysm. The soulless cycles of vengeance would unfortunately continue.

The intruders had what they came for and were on their way home. Taevians could build houses, but the very definition of the word "Taevius" guarranteed that we could never go home. Yet perhaps someday, someone would find a way, just as Brendwolt had found a way to survive here in the first place. Perhaps someday, someone would find a way to heal the wound that had enveloped my people and myself. Perhaps then, we'd all forsake Taevius and finally go home. For now, Taevius--a place with an inescapable past and no future at all--is where I lived.

CHAPTER 9

My Continuing Memories:
From Taevius to Woonhaégen Castle

It seemed I was dreaming again. I saw Sir Trendall and Gairen. We were encamped for the night on a great plain with a few trees silhouetted on the horizon by an orange-red sunset. They seemed to know all that had happened and applied whatever knowledge of healing arts they had to the fresh scars on my face and arms. I forced a weak smile. The knight was bent over a container of some sort that was suspended over a small fire. Now and again, he'd add a particular ingredient from a small sack of provisions lying near his feet. The archer gently massaged bruised areas to stimulate circulation. It was a wonderfully comforting picture.

I closed my eyes, then opened them again. My friends were still there. Perhaps I wasn't dreaming after all. Gairen smiled slightly and I returned the biggest smile the pain of fresh facial wounds would allow. Sir Trendall removed the small container from over the fire, evidently a tea he'd concocted, and added more wood to the flames to protect us from the chilly breeze dancing around our little camp. The archer lifted me to his chest and brought me closer to the warmth of the fire's light, tipping a cup of tea to my lips. I sputtered a second when the sharp, spicy taste first touched my tongue, but the flavor was soothing and the liquid heat relaxing as it flowed deep within me.

We sat there together in silence for a while, smiling at each other, perhaps not knowing what to say, perhaps not needing to say anything at all. The night sky was filled with stars before long. The moon was brilliant. The land around us was quiet and peaceful. It was all beautiful.

I must have drifted off to sleep again, because I opened my eyes to daylight and a feeling of rhythmically but gently bumping along. Gairen smiled down at me, cradling me with one arm and guiding his horse with the other, as the trees of a forest danced quickly by. I turned my head to see Sir Trendall and an extra horse just ahead, moving along at an easy canter.

They paused a while later, just for a moment, at a small clearing just off the path. A few smoldering pieces of wood indicated someone had been there the night before, but neither of my friends gave any indication as to why they'd stopped. A look of recognition passed between them, and a slight smile.

"She's been here and is still somewhere nearby," Trendall said. "How is it that we didn't pass Woonhaégen Castle before reaching this place?"

"Leaving here, we went north," Gairen explained, "but leaving the castle, we went east."

"Should we then detour again to the castle, to discover what the duke may know?"

"The duke seemed sufficiently trustworthy and the lord sufficiently impotent that I expect no danger." The archer grinned momentarily. "But the knowledge the duke possesses may serve both our little friend as well as myself, since we both still seek the lord of Castle Mirus."

The knight nodded his understanding. "I'll see you safely there, but then must be on my way before my own lord counts me as having died in battle somewhere or other. You'll see to the safety of our companion?"

"Yes, I will, but I pray we'll meet again someday, when present journeys are completed and purposes fulfilled."

We rode on to a castle. By now I was strong enough to ride seated across the horse in front of my larger friend, Gairen's strong arms around me, as forests and streams swiftly passed by. The path widened to a sort of road, and, as the sun crept to its western place of rest, a large town came into view. High on a bluff stood a castle with banners flying in the breeze, its towers and battlements catching the last of the sun's glowing rays.

Night had nearly enveloped the land completely when Sir Trendall called to the guard in the gate tower that the duke of Marhaéven's guests had arrived. After a moment's pause, the gate opened and an escort of four mounted soldiers guided us to a large door inside the inner wall. A small page appeared and his eyes shot open at the sight of the knight and archer. He stepped around quickly to get a quick look at me and then rushed off again. He reappeared a moment later to lead us to a courtyard of carefully cultivated flowers and bushes. Torches lit the space from their mountings on the walls.

A man stepped from the shadows, but only far enough for his silhouette to be seen. "You survived."

Sir Trendall nodded, then queried, "the duke of Marhaéven?"

"Yes." The duke bowed slightly. "This is the person of whom you spoke?"

The knight nodded and stepped to the side. I was tempted to retreat to Gairen's protection, but held my ground. The duke's finger remained pointed at me, then curled under as he drew his arm toward his chest and bent to get a better look at me. For a moment I wondered if he might have a cousin who was an alchemist.

"Come, let's go inside, where a fire waits to warm us, and discuss this matter further." The duke turned and moved slowly toward a door on the far side of this courtyard-garden. Sir Trendall strode ahead confidently. I followed but noticed that Gairen seemed ill-at-ease, as was I. Two pages were hastily setting four crude chairs near the hearth, while a third built up the fire. The dancing flames threw eerie shadows onto the walls of the small and somewhat bare room. The door was shut behind us as I took a chair on the far side, the duke chose a seat opposite me, and my two friends sat between us, the knight closest to the duke.

"Before I begin, I'm curious as to your further travel plans," said the duke.

"I have a lord and castle of my own to which..." Sir Trendall began, then stopped and turned to Gairen, briefly glancing downward. The archer's hand had a tight grip on the knight's thigh, but I glanced at Gairen's face and still couldn't figure out what was going on.

"To which we intend to journey in the morning," the archer finished, without glancing at the startled knight. "I'd prefer, however, business before pleasure, as they say. You'd said that you had more to tell us when we returned from Taevius."

A tense moment of silence followed. I looked from face to face.

"Very well," the duke began, "I'll tell you what I know--or rather, what I've been told. Then I'd ask in return that you tell me of all that has occurred since we last spoke."

"Fair enough," Gairen replied.

"To begin with, then," the duke said, "what may be unknown even to you, little one. The origin and a brief history of Taevius."

CHAPTER 10

The Duke of Marhaéven's Chapter

"It was perhaps two, maybe three centuries ago," I began. "Nypothnia was a wilderness inhabited by numerous warring nomads. No common language existed, but certain words were used by most to refer to specific areas. The northwestern swampland was called Phrynondi; the central forest was called Branditi; and the southwestern arid lands were called Syldonia. Lands to the east, however, were avoided for unknown reasons. I suppose the reasons may relate to a history even before the one I'm describing."

"I'm curious whether your story will also include an explanation of how you came to be called the duke of Marhaéven," Sir Trendall interjected.

"No," I replied. "That story will have to wait for another time. In any case, there arose one called Traénon of Syldonia who united the primitive peoples of Nypothnia into a great civilization. He was a truly gifted man, but evidently not altogether wise. He created numerous institutions for the benefit of all: educational and economic systems, systems of government and health-care, systems of transportation and communication, and even systems of law. It was a beautiful and prosperous time. Now it's all but forgotten." I sighed, pausing to recall the glories of this ancient empire. "But Traénon couldn't change the confused nature of mankind. Laws are good, but where laws exist, lawbreakers will be identified as such. So began the perennial question of what to do with criminals. Rehabilitation efforts failed, systems of punishment and reward broke down. In desperation he decided to separate such persons from the main population, hoping to weed out undesirables and form the utopian society he'd envisioned."

I stopped, shook my head a little, and massaged my brow to discourage a tension headache from forming there. "Traénon's scientists were on an expedition, the purpose of which was to explore and to map the eastern frontier. They were traversing the plain there, when a section of earth gave way beneath their mounted leader. In a matter of seconds, an abyss extending from horizon to horizon tore across the plain, claiming the lives of their leader and his mount and forbidding any further exploration in that direction. They'd discovered the chasm where Taevius was to be born, but to this day no one knows what is beyond. Anything you hear is mere speculation."

"So how was Taevius born?" the little misshapen creature interjected.

"Traénon needed a place to send all of those deemed by his system of law to be miscreants."

The air itself felt heavy as I paused to let my last statement sink into the minds of my small audience. "No one had any idea of the harvest that would one day be reaped from such a seedbed, of the way the topographical scar upon the land would eventually etch itself into the lives and even the very soul of Nypothnia's people." I paused. "All rejects of society were collected," I continued, "condemned, and lowered into the abyss that'd been named 'Taevius.' There, they were expected to starve to death unobserved. Obviously, they didn't all starve to death."

"The name 'Taevius'..." Sir Trendall said.

"It's an archaic word, unclearly translated as 'separation' or 'something that is cut away,'" I explained. "At any rate, the idea worked fine for a while, maybe a decade or two, but poor records were kept as to exactly how many had been condemned to Taevius, and no one had ever investigated the mortality rate for those sent there. In the forty-third year of Traénon's reign as sovereign of all of Nypothnia, at the time of the annual celebration of the establishment of law in Nypothnia, a force of incomprehensible proportions was sweeping toward the capital city of Avinngra."

"Avinngra," the knight interrupted, astonished to finally hear the story of the well-known ruins.

"Yes, the name of that city is perhaps the only thing that survived," I said, "with the exception of people living in more remote places, who had sufficient warning to hide themselves." Gairen took a deep breath, remembering himself and Sir Trendall within the hollow tree, as a stunned silence briefly filled the room. "Nearly all knowledge and development was wiped from the land. It was as if they'd never existed, so bitter was the anger of the Taevians at being left to die--and so it has been to this day," I concluded.

The archer cleared his throat. "You mentioned a prophecy when we were here last."

I nodded somewhat despondently. "After you left, I managed to locate and re-analyze that passage in an old manuscript, using the limited collections of books kept in the lower chambers of this castle. Speaking more objectively this time, I'd say that the passage is sufficiently vague that it could refer to anyone bringing any kind of relief from the oppression of the oppressive hordes. I suspect it was some wistful poet's longing for salvation from the yearly onslaught. The verse really doesn't express anything more than the belief that someday someone would cause the yearly nightmare to cease."

I sighed, finished with expounding upon Taevian history. "It's your turn," I said, breaking the silence again. "What transpired during your visit to Taevius and how did you manage to rescue your little friend from such a foe?"

Gairen remained quiet, with a deeply thoughtful expression upon his face, as Sir Trendall recounted the little one's rescue, the latter adding details from his perspective whenever they were helpful. At the end of the knight's narrative, a low whistle escaped from my lips.

"So in actuality, any of the three of you might've fulfilled this prophecy," I suggested.

I spoke with Sir Trendall further about the prophecy, but like Gairen the little one remained strangely quiet now and had a far-away look in his eyes. I thought perhaps we'd made a mistake by reminding him of his Taevian childhood in some less tolerable way.

The archer suddenly broke his lingering silence. "The facts remain that we don't know how much of the city of Taevius was destroyed, how many of its citizens survived, or even whether this will incite a greater reprisal from them against the rest of Nypothnia."

59

As the awful truth of his words seeped into our minds, I and the knight looked from one to another and also to the little one. I had no way of knowing how Taevians would respond to such a cataclysmic avalanche, especially one caused by a non-Taevian. No such thing had ever happened there before, if the remaining historical records were still accurate.

"Now more than ever," Gairen interrupted the many thoughts, "it's essential that we find those who survived the attack on Castle Mirus. The king has knowledge of arcane arts that may be the greatest hope for all of us. Have you any knowledge or heard any rumor concerning my lord, King Treston of Castle Mirus?"

I swallowed hard, took a deep breath, and spoke in a calmer voice. "To begin with, it's believed in certain circles that he's the last living descendant of Traénon."

The knight and the archer were clearly dumbfounded by this announcement.

I continued. "It's therefore fair to presume that he has the greatest existing collection of recorded knowledge from the time of civilization, from before the dark, feudal time in which we live. As to his current whereabouts, no one with whom I've spoken has heard anything that's certain." I briefly waited for a reaction. "However, I've made a few speculations based only on logic."

I stopped again, not knowing whether to continue. Everyone was still staring at me. "He'd most likely have tried to reach the one place that even the Taevians would be least likely to go." My voice trailed off to a whisper at the end.

"Well, where for goodness sake?" Sir Trendall demanded.

With a deep sigh, I softly answered. "The far side of the chasm, beyond Taevius."

CHAPTER 11

My Continuing Memories:
The Quest for King Treston

Beyond Taevius. What lay beyond Taevius? Even spending my entire childhood within the dividing city itself, I had no answer to this question. Danger? Rewards? Perhaps nothing but more vast, empty grasslands?

"Come, little friend," Sir Trendall said. "It is time to rest, that we may wake refreshed and prepared for the day to come." Gairen's eyes were already heavy as we followed the duke of Marhaéven and a page to sleeping chambers in another part of the castle.

It had been decided that the duke would join us, bringing three servants and twelve guards, on the quest for the king of Castle Mirus. All would have horses so that we could move quickly, since we'd need to journey far to the south in order to circumvent the chasm. We couldn't go north, because the duke had what he considered to be a reliable report of an extremely hostile climate there. In choosing to go south, however, it was probable that we'd need to go all the way to the Bay of Brendwolt. It was also quite possible that the chasm had in fact, split Nypothnia completely into two pieces. Whatever was on the other side had presumably had no contact with anyone on this side of the chasm for over two hundred years.

Dark clouds, rain, and thunder rolled in at dawn. An ominous silence hung over our small company for hours after leaving the castle. Then we emerged onto the vast plain and the rain stopped. Thick, grey clouds hung overhead for as far as any of us could see. It was difficult to triangulate the sun's position, but finally a southeastern heading was established and the group's morale improved a bit. The clouds pulled apart late in the afternoon, giving a pleasant view of the sun sinking into the far western edge of the plain. Hours had passed since we'd seen

61

even a single tree. With the day's light fading quickly, we chose a site randomly and set up camp for the night.

A small fire was quickly built, but shielded to make it less visible from a distance. The plain seemed desolate enough, but none could say what or who might be out there in the vast darkness. We ate our evening meal in relative silence, with minor discussions in low whispers between the duke and the knight. I noticed that a number of the guards were staring at me with puzzled expressions. I finished eating a piece of bread and some strange sort of apple before deciding to strike up a conversation. "So what are your names?"

"Drinlar."

"Nartok."

"Ehrgsos."

"Eftral."

"Nifgon."

"Verbont."

"Velarso."

"Aldern."

"Esstrol."

"Ahdrynne."

"Riomar."

"Roshto."

They were young men, strong and daring but without the advantage of experience possessed by the duke, who claimed to have seen more military conflicts than anyone could ever wish to see. I grew more impressed with the duke's controlled wisdom with each passing day and suspected that he was older than he appeared to be, though his condescension and subtle arrogance were a bit annoying.

No one could say for certain just how much risk our expedition involved. We might be the only persons there, and then again we might encounter hostile forces with abilities we'd never even imagined. We might search for a week or for months or we might never find the king we sought at all. Looking at the twelve guards, it was fair to ask but impossible to answer whether all or any of them would return home alive.

The twelve shared stories of families and loved ones to whom they hoped to return, but recognized as well that it was for the safety of those loved ones that they were here. Every family in Nypothnia had lost someone to the Taevian invasions at some time or other. On the other hand, in the light of recent events, I didn't know whether my family was still alive or not, or whether my escape had made my family as good as dead to me. Obviously I had my doubts.

"So what about you?" Nartok grinned optimistically.

"Yeah, what's your family like?" said Ehrgsos.

"Do you have a girl waiting for you somewhere?" Drinlar asked impishly.

Slowly and solemnly, as if weighing each word, Velarso said, "why are you shaped so strangely?"

His eyes met mine for a long moment and, as the dim light from the flames of our small fire danced across our faces, I prepared to begin again with the tale of my first escape from Taevius.

Gairen burst into our midst, smothering the fire with dust and dirt. "Grab your swords," he whispered.

The horses started stamping about, making nervous noises as the three servants fought to calm and quiet them. A sliver of moonlight lit the plain as the guards fanned out around the camp. The wind began to swirl strangely. Suddenly the campfire flickered to life again. Gairen started toward it, then jerked away.

"Hello."

The archer dove to the ground, rolled to the side, and came up with a small dagger raised.

Sir Trendall whirled to face the voice. "Masra," the knight said, relieved. "It's you."

"Yes," an old woman replied. "I said that you'd see me again when the need arose."

The guards had encircled the camp, their swords drawn, their faces bearing expressions of blank confusion. The duke stared at the woman now seated by the fire with cold calculation. Then he circled and sat opposite her.

"How did you get here?" the duke began.

"Irrelevant," Masra waved the question off.

"Are you who I think you might be?" said the duke.

"Who is it that you consider me to be?" Masra said slyly.

"She who was to have been the queen of Castle Mirus," the duke replied.

Masra's small smile fell from her face as the mouths of the archer and the knight dropped open in astonishment.

"You're the duke of Marhaéven," she said, "as honest as one can be who's consistently motivated by selfish interests. You'd do well to learn from your travelling companions. For the present, you're not my concern. The little refugee from Taevius is. Be sure that you do no evil toward him, nor use him disrespectfully for your own gain. You will have opportunity to do so."

Masra paused, a chilling gaze fixed upon the duke. He attempted an appearance of bravado.

"To the rest of you, I suggest that you be careful not to trust the duke implicitly. Yes, I am she who would've been queen of Castle Mirus had the Taevians not attacked when they did. I would've born the king an heir, and may yet, if he can be found and all affairs set right. If not, Traénon's line will perish from Nypothnia and the time of civilization might never return." Masra stopped, turned to the guards, and bid them lower their weapons before continuing, "True it is that he who would've been my husband is now in the lands beyond Taevius, but something interferes and I cannot clearly perceive any details with which to assist you. Only be sure that you don't ever give up the search."

The duke shrugged. "So what help have you come to offer?"

"I've been able to determine that despite the barrenness you see here, there are people and even cities on the other side of the chasm. Much can be learned from them." She paused. "The chasm extends southward all the way to the Bay of Brendwolt, but there's a small village of seafaring people on the sandy shore that connects the two halves of Nypothnia."

"Why couldn't we go north?" Nifgon asked.

"The northern coast of Nypothnia is extremely cold, although the chasm ends a distance of at least two days' ride

64

from the Bay of Gendaro. Nevertheless, a few people do live there, despite the severe climate."

Masra began again where she'd been interrupted. "Those on the southern coast at the end of the chasm will help you in whatever way you ask, but they never consent to leave their village for more than a day, no matter what the reason."

"Why's that?" asked Drinlar.

"Of that, I'm uncertain, but be sure that you don't ask. They're most friendly when left to their own chosen ways, whether or not those ways seem right to you. Pass through their village in peace, pursuing your own goal."

Masra stood quickly as if she'd heard something. The guards spun around, swords raised, alternately peering into the darkness and looking back at the old woman. Strangely, she seemed to have grown slightly younger during the discourse around the fire.

"I wish you well and trust that we'll speak again before long." She turned and in a moment was gone. The wind stirred the air around our camp once again and then fell silent.

The duke looked to the knight for a moment. "So you've met the old woman who is not so old as myself?"

"Can you explain yourself more clearly, sir?" Sir Trendall replied with an irritated edge to his voice.

The duke focused on the fire's flames as he remembered. "She was a reasonably beautiful young lady when first we met and I would've taken her for myself when she sought refuge for the night at Woonhaégen Castle, but she had eyes only for a king she'd never seen but who'd invited her to visit him. It wasn't her outward beauty that drew all men toward her, as much as her sharp wit and benevolent personality. Here was a potent woman. I suppose that most men find a little competition exciting, now and then."

"But she appeared so very old," countered Aldern.

"Yes. That's unfortunate, but I understand that it isn't irreversible. She did meet the king of Castle Mirus and none were ever better matched intellectually than those two. King Treston had access to more knowledge than she, so for a while it was a kind of teacher-student relationship, but she excelled in true goodness; she was the heart to his head and an emotional bond of unusual intensity developed. I suppose, in a sense, they became each other's life-energy. A little more than two years ago, she left to retrieve her belongings from her father's castle. Her plan was afterwards to return to Castle Mirus to become the king's bride and queen, but she found her father murdered and the castle razed to its foundations by Taevian marauders. In great sadness she fled to Castle Mirus, only to find it also razed to its foundations. Yet it's said that she found something in the rubble, a message of some sort from King Treston, and also the thing that gives her the inexplicable abilities you've witnessed. But as to your question; the longer the two lovers are separated, the more quickly they age."

I dared to speak my impression. "It appeared to me that the aging process reversed slightly during the time she was with us this evening. Was this my own misperception?"

The duke's eyes grew wide momentarily. "I suspect it could only mean that the king was somehow making himself spiritually present; which, if true, indicates that on some level he's aware of us as well, though possibly not of her. If he knew Masra was here, I expect he would've appeared to claim her as his bride at last."

The camp grew quiet upon hearing that speculation and all began peering into the blackness, wondering again exactly who and how many might be silently observing our small company. Apparently our journey was not simply our own private little experience.

The guards took turns watching over the camp as the night dragged on. I felt somewhat rested in the morning, but continued to wrestle with the puzzling events of the previous evening. Evidently Sir Trendall and Gairen had met this woman before, judging by the few scattered comments they made while eating a morning meal.

We rode all day, the landscape unchanging. The sky finally cleared, however, and when the sun had gone the expansive blackness was covered with stars, like diamonds spilled across black velvet.

How many, I wondered, had never seen the stars, living their lives in caves? How many had gone from birth to death neither knowing nor understanding how beautiful things beyond their perception and understanding could be? Then again, it's a fair question to ask why some find transcendent things to be magnificent, awe-inspiring, and at least somewhat potentially good, while others find that all that's beyond their understanding to be frightening, dangerous, and evil.

Esstrol interrupted my musings to remind me that they'd not heard the story of my family the night before, being understandably distracted by Masra's visit. I nodded and joined the others around the fire.

CHAPTER 12

Drinlar's Chapter

"I was born deformed," the little misshapen person began, staring into the fire, "thus bringing great shame to my father in the eyes of the other warriors in the village. My father blamed my mother and must have punished her harshly, because she became increasingly withdrawn as time went on. Perhaps it was also her own inability to accept that she'd given birth to one such as I. The others in Taevius usually acted as if I wasn't even there, just an invisible spirit with no relevance to anything. At first, the others close to my own age taunted me as they would a caged animal or a freak, which I guess I was, or am. Later, even they ignored me. The rotting firewood near the hearth received more attention than I did. Even the half-wild dogs that ran loose throughout the city grew bored with me."

He paused a moment and I interrupted. "Obviously, they greatly underestimated your worth."

"I agree with Drinlar," Ahdrynne said quickly. "I haven't known you that long, but already I'm quite taken by your loving spirit, your smile, and the way your eyes twinkle in the firelight."

"I don't think I'm exaggerating," the little one replied. "Though I'm sure this must sound like a 'poor little me' kind of speech. I tell you these things simply because this is how I remember them. I do find, however, that each time I call forth such memories, that I notice other details I hadn't noticed before. Obviously the parts of these events which I remember are not all that these events included."

The moon's luminescence began to drape the landscape in shades of royal blue. Gairen's eyes sparkled within a deeply thoughtful expression, but not one which included a smile.

The small one continued. "The village priests couldn't seem to decide whether I was evil, an insignificant freak, or perhaps whether it was something I'd grow out of eventually. Not once did they encourage me to think of myself as special in some way--not that I am. Or maybe...I mean...I'm just me--just a person who never fit in anywhere. In any case, I'd occasionally be beaten, I was once forced to undergo some strange rite of exorcism, but most often I was just ignored which was certainly easier to deal with than the first two. You asked me to speak of my family, but I'm afraid there's not much to tell."

"Certainly there's more than you think," said Gairen, "That's what you suggested a few moments ago.".

The little one shrugged and began again by relating a few details, then concluded, "That's really all I remember--at least for now."

Gairen's face took on a knowing look and he responded quietly but so that everyone could hear, "Perhaps for now. In time, I suspect that much more will be remembered."

The little one tipped his face to the ground, then looked up again as he continued. "The priests of Taevius were strange men appointed to guard ancient mysteries that most of the people have forgotten and for which they therefore seem generally unconcerned. Those with political aspirations in Taevius, however, need to familiarize themselves with such things because the religious matters of the town may be unknown, but they are never totally disregarded. The priest is as much a fact of their existence as the sun and moon; the villages have nothing to do with them whatsoever, but would strongly resist their removal."

"I'd often go off alone to wander through the cavernous cliffs around Taevius to try and sort out my thoughts and feelings. One of the priests, named Droknoto, evidently knew of my periodic escapes. I'd gone to my favorite place late one morning, a particular cave on the far wall of the chasm, and sat watching the people wander through the streets below, when a hand touched my shoulder. I whirled around. It was Droknoto. Evidently he'd been hiding further back in the shadows when I'd arrived. He was smiling strangely with his hand outstretched toward me. He moved around, blocking the small cave's opening, still saying nothing. He was easily twice my size and had evidently been a strong warrior before being chosen for the priesthood by the old highpriest, Orveld. I backed away. He

70

seized my clothes at the shoulder and flung me onto my back roughly. I could hear my heart pounding. His left hand felt cold on my small chest, reaching under the thin hide wrap I wore. He untied the thongs of my clothes and threw them aside. He knelt over me and exposed himself completely. I could hardly breathe. I opened my mouth and his hand clamped down over it, silencing any sound I would've made. 'This is every Taevian boy's passage to manhood,' he said, 'consider yourself lucky to receive the rite earlier than most.' He would've forced himself upon me then, but a venomous snake as big as his arm and three times as long appeared by the wall, raised itself high off the floor and flared its neck-folds as if about to strike. Droknoto rolled away in fear, snatched his priestly robes and scrambled down the ledge toward Taevius."

"I just lay there, staring at the snake, feeling somehow relieved. The snake stared back, then lowered itself to the floor of the cave again. It came closer, very close. I felt numb and exhausted. We stared at each other for another long moment. Then it just turned and slithered back into the cave's gloomy depths. I lay there naked for a few moments, the gentle winds caressing my body, a strange but peaceful feeling. I moved my arm to get up and suddenly became aware of my physical body again. It was like waking from a particularly intense dream."

I shook my head and looked around the circle of faces, remembering where I was as well. I had no trouble imagining what I would've done if I'd been there instead of the snake, when that priest had behaved so evilly. The little one's hands were shaking a little. The archer's jaw was tense. The knight sat a few paces away, holding his face in his hands, his elbows resting on his knees. The duke seemed emotionally detached, drawing random lines in the dusty earth with a small stick of firewood.

Riomar broke the silence. "How was it that you survived such an awful place?"

The little one and he stared at each other in silence. Finally the little one looked away, shook his head and shrugged, before responding, "I felt numb for a few days, somehow convinced that everyone who looked at me would know what had happened. I felt ashamed, but I didn't know why."

71

I was about to interject a reminder of his innocence when he swiped a tear from his eye and jumped back into telling the story. "Some eight or nine years ago, I discovered a strange old man in one of the caves more distant from Taevius. I wouldn't have believed anyone lived out there. His long grey hair hung down to his waist like dry strands of grass that had been left in the sun too long, and his eyes were dark and sunken. His clothes were more ragged than anything I'd seen in Taevius. He also had a beard, unlike anyone in Taevius, where it was the custom to keep the skin of the face shaved smooth."

"He stretched a long, bony finger toward me and his lips began to quiver," the little one continued. "He began to mumble something, his voice like dry branches rustling against stone. He paused and then repeated what he'd said, but still I failed to understand. I just stood there staring at him. He stared back at me. His arm lowered as he sighed and began to hum something. There'd never been any music in Taevius, not real music anyway. It was an intriguing sound. The tones seemed to rise and fall like the surging and ebbing strength of the wind and the swirling of dust in the streets. Then he stopped and beckoned me closer to sit opposite of him on the dusty cave floor. I did so."

The archer looked up suddenly, anxiously, distracting the rest of us. The little one smiled to reassure him. Gairen seemed to want to ask something, but waited for the story to continue instead.

"He spoke in melancholy tones. I understood at least some of the words this time. He wasn't from Taevius. He'd come there seeking to bring a different beauty and truth with which the city was unfamiliar, but he hadn't been understood and thus had been driven out. Yet he chose to stay nearby, learning by observation and spending hours doing something he called prayer, hoping always for something good to happen. I found his words strange but barely comprehensible. He began a long and fascinating tale of lands to the west, of languages and peoples I'd never imagined existed."

"A sudden swirl of dust born by the wind warned of an evening storm. I stumbled to my feet and with a last look at the old man's dark eyes, I hurried out and scurried back to Taevius.

I tossed fitfully in my sleep all night long, and in the morning hurried back to learn more if I could."

"The old man smiled this time when I appeared. He had a tiny charcoal fire at his side with a few last pieces of what I think had been a snake, hanging from a small spit above it. I must have made a face because he chuckled loudly. Somehow, the idea of having snake for breakfast didn't appeal to me."

Other guards around the circle broke into a mumbled debate over the taste of snake meat, Verbont being especially vocal about the magnificent taste of the meat, when properly prepared. I chuckled as the little one made an unpleasant face and shook his head before continuing.

"He began to teach me the languages of the peoples in faraway lands that he'd described the day before, and also this strange phenomena he called music. In a week's time, he became perhaps the only friend I had in the whole world."

Gairen shifted his footing uncomfortably at this announcement.

"The old man's clothing was strange to me at the time, being made from fibers rather than hide. One day he gave me a large, heavy piece of this material, the dark brown cloak that I still carry with me thanks to my two friends." He smiled at Gairen and Sir Trenall. "I hid it in the back of a cave nearer to my father's house because I dared not bring it home for him to find."

The eyes of many of our company were getting heavy, I noticed, and gestured to the little story teller. Sir Trendall spoke up and affirmed my silent suggestion. "It's late and time to rest," He turned to the little one and added, "We'd like to hear more at another time." The little one nodded quickly.

We established the order of night watch, found whatever spot on the ground seemed most comfortable and rolled into our blankets. The duke, however, used the added padding of the saddle blankets, explaining that he couldn't possibly get any rest without them. Gairen shook his head and rolled onto his side to face away from the duke.

In a few minutes, the only sound was heavy breathing. Only the little one, I and Eftral, who had the first watch, remained awake. Eftral looked toward the little one and smiled. His smile was immediately returned, before he turned his attention to the surrounding darkness and his duties.

Everyone was up early except for the duke and our smallest companion. The little one seemed to be genuinely resting, so we chose not to disturb him until necessary. The duke was snoring quietly, but he was generally less irritating when he was unconscious. Gairen and Sir Trendall had half of the camp's provisions strapped to the backs of saddles on horses already. Nartok and I were saddling the last of the horses, when the servants decided to awaken the duke and offer him a small breakfast.

"Why in such a hurry this morning?" the duke complained.

"There is a crispness to the breeze that foreshadows a heavy frost," replied Gairen, not turning his eyes from the bundle his fingers were nimbly strapping to the back of Aldern's mount. "We must move quickly in case the frost intends to grow to a freezing storm."

With that admonition, our company was underway in moments, moving at a brisk canter. We kept a steady pace for all of the next six days. Bit by bit, the coldness in the wind diminished. The sky cleared and the heat of the sun began beating upon us instead, inviting the removal of excess cloaks, caps, and clothing. By the eighth day of our journey, the forest surrounding Woonhaégen Castle was far behind us and the sun's heat had become so intense that the horses began to lather. We slowed to a walk. When the sun was high and the shadows short, Gairen called the company to an abrupt halt.

"Listen," he said.

Faintly, I heard the soft hushing sound of waves tumbling over themselves onto a sandy beach.

"There," shouted Nifgon with obvious delight. "The mist rises like a fog."

Gairen turned his mount to the right a bit, heading in the direction Nifgon indicated. The horses sensed the water as well and began to run. The land sloped downward and soon the horses were kicking up sand as they argued with their riders for the freedom to immerse themselves in the surf. A low outcropping of dark stone was chosen to receive the company's belongings while horses and men were set loose to refresh themselves in the sun and sand and surf. Clothing was discarded and I'm sure anyone watching from a distance would've seen only a bunch of children at play.

Only the duke refrained from the relaxed, happy moments there. He seemed preoccupied with something but wouldn't disclose his concerns to the rest of us.

The little one seemed hesitant, almost afraid of something. I glanced to Velarso, trying to phrase a question by a facial expression and a sideways nod of my head toward our small companion. He understood and took a few slow steps toward our little friend, then smiled and nodded to him. The little one smiled back and pulled off his clothing, then scurried toward the water's edge. The other guards noticed what was happening and stopped their playing to look. The little naked young man stopped to look around at all of them, standing in the shallow water near the shore with incoming waves swirling about their legs. I suppose to one with different proportions we must have seemed like classically beautiful men, thanks to rigorous physical training. I couldn't help but sense a sad sort of longing in the little one's expression.

Velarso grinned and ran toward him then, scooped him up, raced back into the water, and threw him toward Riomar. The little friend fell below the surface in a big splash and came up again in Riomar's arms sputtering. The others burst out laughing and a wild aquatic wrestling match with eighteen contenders ensued.

Yes, I'd say it was a truly wonderful day.

CHAPTER 13

My Continuing Memories:
Moments with the Guards

The waves surged around us as we wrestled playfully. Ehrgsos moved to tackle Eftral, but was himself caught by an incoming wave and thrown under. Sputtering with surprise, he burst through the receding surf in time to see Roshto diving toward him. Then they both went under in a tangle of flailing arms and legs.

I was sitting on Velarso's shoulders, since the water was deeper here and in addition to being so short I'd never learned to swim, having been raised in an arid environment. I rested my hands on his head, his wet golden brown hair glistening in the sun. The wind and waves washed over me from time to time and I became aware of the pleasant feeling of my skin against Velarso's. It was a sort of connection that I'd never felt before, perhaps as much spiritual as physical. I wondered whether he felt it too, by the way he looked up and smiled from time to time. He had grey-green eyes; I hadn't noticed that before.

Nartok took it upon himself to stir things up a bit more. He climbed onto Nifgon's shoulders and they charged and sent both Velarso and me floundering onto our backs. Aldern's strong hands lifted me up again as I shook my head furiously back and forth, trying to get the water out of my nose. Velarso shot out of the water like a porpoise, landing on Nartok and pushing him underwater for a moment. Nartok popped up first, a few feet away from where he'd been pushed under. Then Ahdrynne appeared behind him, hooking his arms under and around Nartok's shoulders, rendering him completely vulnerable. Before Velarso could respond, however, Verbont and Eftral seized the opportunity to begin rapidly slapping Nartok's stomach, turning it a bright pink, to the amusement of the rest of us. Nartok protested, but burst out laughing as he struggled, leaping upon his assailants the moment he was released. Then

77

someone discovered that Drinlar was very ticklish and the water churned tremendously as he became the focus of friendly torture.

Aldern passed me back to Velarso and the three of us started toward the shore. Aldern got there first and threw himself down on the sand, tipping his blond head back with his eyes closed in contentment. Velarso swung me from his shoulders into the shallow surf when we were close to the shore. The sand was unexpectedly hot when I stepped beyond the water's reach and Velarso laughed softly at the way I hopped about for a moment. He lay down next to Aldern to dry in the sun, inviting me with a gesture to lie between them. A strange, warm emotion fluttered through me as I sat down and lay back onto the sand.

I closed my eyes. The muscles in my back trembled slightly from the heat of the sand, trembled and then relaxed. Turning my head to the side, I opened my eyes to see Velarso looking back at me with a small smile on his face. He lifted his arm and pulled me to his side, his arm under my head and around my shoulders; then he closed his eyes again. A warm, safe feeling flooded through me.

A cool breeze tickled me awake. I lifted my head from Velarso's chest to see him smiling contentedly at me, the orange glow of early evening bathing his features. I rubbed the sleep from my eyes as he stood and moved away, returning a moment later with our clothes. Drinlar and Aldern had already dressed and were preparing an evening meal for our company. The last of the guards were dressing when I noticed Gairen returning from somewhere further to the east along the shore. Sir Trendall and the duke were with him.

A refreshed group of men gathered around the fire that evening, to sup and discuss the next day's travel.

"We walked for an hour at least and saw no sign of the village described by Masra," Sir Trendall began, "but if our navigation to this spot has been accurate, then it can't be more than a long day's ride before we reach that place and begin our journey inland again."

"The horses are refreshed," Nifgon commented. "They should do well even if the ride tomorrow turns out to be somewhat long."

Gairen nodded. "We did find a small inlet or cove where there might be a fair harvest of fish to be caught. We'll pause there for an hour or two tomorrow, to supplement our provisions."

"Forgive my ignorance," said Esstrol, "having been raised inland as I was, but how exactly does one catch a fish?"

With much innuendo and a smirk on his face, Ahdrynne replied," You just have to have the right bait."

Interrupting a burst of laughter from the other guards, the duke concluded, "All that being said, I have nothing more to add, except to ask whether anything unusual occurred during our brief absence." His eyes scanned the circle of shaking heads. "Fine then." He gestured to us to begin the evening meal.

I'd dismissed all notion of potential danger in the days ahead during the recreational hours I'd spent with the guards in the waters of the Bay of Brendwolt. Gairen and Sir Trendall had played along with the rest of us at first, but were obviously more concerned with the future of this expedition and so had joined the duke after a short swim. I didn't really know what to expect in the days ahead, but I was happy enough not to worry about it for a while. Good or bad, it would all be dealt with in due time.

Velarso interrupted my thoughts. "Shall we continue with your story, my friend?" His eyes sparkled in the firelight, as he smiled a little in anticipation.

I nodded, then paused to ask, "Where was I?"

"You'd just received a brown cloak from the curious man within the cave," Roshto replied, bringing a large spoonful of thick stew to his lips.

"Okay." I gathered my thoughts. "Well, I can't remember much more to tell of that strange old man, except for the day I discovered a rock slide where the cave had been. I don't know whether he escaped or not. In any case, I've never seen him again. I was deeply saddened by the loss of my friend, but perhaps he'd taught me everything that he could. People seem to come in and out of my life as if according to some plan. I guess I'm learning to trust that wherever I am, no matter what happens, someone will be there to help." I looked around at all these new friends, wishing there was some way to adequately thank them.

79

"I stood there a long time, staring at the rubble, trying to remember all the things he'd told me, trying to understand what exactly I should do. I suppose the answer was obvious," I said. "I remember that the wind caressed my cheek in a new way, it seemed, and I turned to make my way back to Taevius for one more night. I had no plan, no map, and no provisions, only a feeling that I needed to go south and west."

"I wandered off toward the caves the next morning with nothing but the clothes I wore and retrieved the brown cloak from where I'd hidden it within a cave about halfway between Taevius and the cave within which the strange old man had lived. No one paid any attention to me anyway, so leaving was simply a matter of my own choice and not so much of an actual escape. Before leaving, however, I went to the pile of rubble that marked the spot where the bearded man's cave had been. I stared a moment before turning to go, but a reflection of the sun's light caught my eye. Barely covered with dust at the far side of the pile lay a ring with a curious inscription on it. I suppose it must have belonged to the old man. I slipped it over one of my fingers and it almost fit, but I lost it again while scaling the chasm walls."

Sir Trendall's head jerked up at the mention of the chasm walls.

The duke stared at me intensely. "The inscription, do you remember the inscription, what it looked like, whether there were any words, anything about it at all?"

I was puzzled and shook my head slowly. "No, nothing comes to mind."

The duke stared at me for another moment, then dismissed the matter with a wave of his hand and turned to stare into the fire, pondering something.

"It was nearly dark when I reached the top of the chasm," I continued. "The moon was obscured by thick clouds. But the night was warm and quiet. In that the chasm lies like a giant gouge in the earth from north to south, I figured that if I just headed as directly away from it as possible that I'd wind up in the lands described to me. In retrospect, I obviously had no idea how far it would be before I reached those lands."

A couple of people chuckled.

"You had no provisions," Ehrgsos said intensely. "How ever did you make it?"

"How?" I shrugged. "Just barely. I'd never gone without food for so long before and I pray that I'll never have to do so again."

"Would you like some more stew?" Esstrol said, half seriously, half in jest. "There's still a little left."

"No, thank you," I chuckled, accompanied by numerous grins around the circle. "I suppose it might have been a week, maybe a little more, I don't know, when I finally came to a village. Mostly I just walked whenever I was awake. The land had seemed less flat the further I went and there were even trees scattered around like isolated sentries after a while."

"The village was deep in a much more forested valley, barely visible from the ridge upon which I found myself. High on the ridge on the far side of the valley was a medium-small-sized castle. I headed down into the valley and the forest around me grew dark very quickly. I found a well-worn path after a bit of stumbling and the night began to fill with strange sounds. Yet there was a kind of rhythm and harmony to this music of the night," I told them.

"The path seemed to wind along the valley floor in basically one direction but definitely not in a straight line. I felt my way along, testing each step with my feet because the night had grown so dark. The moon peered through the scattered holes in the black tent of tree branches above me, offering some comfort in what was becoming a frightening place. A small animal burst from hiding each time I ventured too close, scaring me as much as itself as it raced away into the darkness."

"Then I began to hear voices and music from somewhere in the distance and also a little above me. A light breeze came up and bore a cool, sweet smell and a faint, gurgling noise. Just ahead the moon lit up a rough log bridge over a small brook. On the far side were a couple of small houses whose windows were tightly shuttered. Behind the shutters I heard snoring. I glanced around and started across the bridge. The moon seemed to glow more brightly than ever, through the opening in the trees above the brook." I paused, noting the moon to be somewhat bright tonight as well. "The water was relatively still where it ran under the bridge. The gurgling noise was caused by some large rocks in its bed further downstream. I glanced downward when I was nearly halfway across and almost lost my balance. A creature peered up at me. I stared back. It didn't move. Gods and goddesses, it was me." I paused, took a deep breath, and sighed. "I'd never seen my reflection before. No wonder my parents tried not to look at me too much, with misshapen features such as those I saw. I truly was a freak. I slumped to the log floor of the bridge. In comparison to others I looked so wrong, but I'd never felt wrong before, at least not in the way I did on that bridge then. How could I go to the people in these new lands now, looking as I did, and still do? I stared at the reflection, overwhelmed."

I trembled slightly, recalling the first moment of self-discovery.

Velarso came up behind me with my brown cloak and wrapped his arm around my shoulders and the cloak around both of us. "I can honestly say that I've never met anyone who looks as you do," he said, "but if others have told you by their actions that your appearance is wrong, then I'd like you to know by my actions that your appearance is exactly right for you. Appearances are neither good nor bad; they simply are what they are. What you are, is my friend; what I am, is your friend."

Aldern reached over, patted my knee a couple times, and smiled. A few others nodded.

"I know that and I've never been more blessed than to have all of you as friends," I replied. "You've asked to hear my story and so I tell it to you, even though it's a story of much difficulty and pain, as well as of eventual triumph and joy. I feel unable to adequately express my gratitude to you for the happiness of this day that we've just shared. As much as we have become each others' friends, I notice that we have also become channels of healing for each other."

Velarso gave me an extra hug, smiled, and nodded for me to continue.

At that moment, however, the duke stepped between my audience and me. "Tomorrow will be yet another adventure. It's time to prepare by getting a good night's rest."

Perhaps a bit reluctantly, we retired to our blankets, spread around the fire on the soft sand of the beach.

Ehrgsos caught my attention as we were going and whispered, "I never knew my father. He was killed in one of the Taevian raids while defending our small farm. My mother and I were hiding in a corner of the barn under the hay and the rogues wanted to set it on fire. They were unsuccessful, but only because of my father's sacrifice." He paused and swallowed. "His last muffled cry of pain still rings in my ears." He paused again, then turned his eyes to mine. "How intriguing that I volunteered to help a person of Taevian descent while in pursuit of an indirect cause of the final demise of the Taevian forces-- such a curiously complex situation." He stared at me in a brooding sort of way for a moment.

I sensed the pain of his loss but could think of little to say. "I'm sorry," I whispered.

I reached up. He bent down. We held each other briefly with both forgetfulness and remembrance.

CHAPTER 14

Nifgon's Chapter

"Nifgon," the duke called. "You bring up the rear, making sure we leave nothing behind." When he had turned his attention to other matters, I looked to Sir Trendall quickly, wondering if the expedition's leadership was in agreement. He nodded silently, evidently deciding to humor the duke's abiding preference for being in charge. I tied the last few things to the back of my saddle as the expedition got underway again.

The morning began with a brief ride, perhaps a half hour, to the small inlet or cove of which Gairen had spoken. Sir Trendall didn't want to delay there even one minute more than necessary, but we were poorly equipped for fishing and spent most of our time in great frustration. Ahdrynne had been born and raised on the western coast of Nypothnia and thus knew more about fishing than all the rest of us combined, but had none of the equipment with which he was used to working. Our attempts would've been amusing, if repetitious failure hadn't made them so infuriating. Swords, clubs, and even our bare hands all proved inadequate. Gairen did far better than the rest of us. Once he learned to allow for the visual distortion of the water, he secured a good two dozen fish by firing his arrows from astride a fairly tall tree that leaned out over the water. "There's another one for you, Nifgon," the archer called to me. Each successful hit from Gairen's bow brought cheers of approval. We resumed our trip in a triumphant mood.

The topography of the beach didn't seem to change at all as we rode along in the warm morning light. When our shadows lay small and dark beneath us, we stopped for a midday meal and decided on the fish we'd caught, rather than opening the provisions we'd brought from the castle. Ahdrynne gave expert instruction on the culinary preparation of our medium-large specimens, rendering the results of our amateur efforts deliciously successful.

85

As the others readied our things for further travel along the beach, I overheard the little one talking with Ahdrynne, who was savoring his last bit of fish. "So why didn't you stay with your family? Did the life of a fisherman not please you?"

"My parents worked hard from dawn to dusk, dragging fish from the sea. My older brother, younger sister, and I helped out as soon as we learned to walk." Ahdrynne finished the last morsel and stood up. "There is an intriguing and mysterious poetry to the tightly interwoven lives of humanity and nature in a seafaring town, as if both teeter on the edge of survival, whether they actually do or not." They walked to Ahdrynne's horse. "I suppose it just didn't suit me. I don't remember having a strong reason for leaving, but my parents didn't even have time to say good-bye."

There was an emptiness in his eyes visible even from where I stood several paces away. I was going to interrupt to encourage him to go back someday, but I suppose that if he did he'd find his family so busy working that they wouldn't have time to even say, hello.

Ahdrynne turned back to our little friend. "Not all seafaring families are like that, but mine was." He paused thoughtfully. "Soon you'll see a seafaring town for yourself. The smell of the salty air and the fish being pulled ashore and sorted and cleaned and smoked." He paused again, a faraway look in his eyes, and smiled a little.

The duke's voice interrupted. "All right, let's get moving before any more daylight escapes us." Ahdrynne raised the little one onto his horse, smiled again and turned to his own horse, the curls of his sandy-brown hair dancing in the gentle wind that swirled around all of us.

It was perhaps three or four hours later when I heard a strange, metallic music in the distance. Gairen pulled up short, stopping all the rest behind him, and listened intently. He led us forward at a walk to a rocky outcropping, then peered around it. "There it is," the archer murmured. "Everyone keep in mind what Masra said."

We moved slowly around the outcropping and down the beach. None of the villagers seemed to notice us until we were almost even with the first house, a small, curiously shaped dwelling made of rocks and shells and seaweed. An old woman wearing a pale green shawl about her head and shoulders appeared from behind a house just ahead, clapped her hands and smiled, then chuckled loudly. Then she turned quickly and hobbled back out of sight. We continued forward, passing the first house before a group of men appeared in front of us. Most of the men were somewhat stocky and plump, though the woman had looked exceedingly thin.

The men were all dressed pretty much the same, but one stepped to the front and made some strange, guttural noises. We just looked at each other. Another stepped to the front and made sounds that were somewhat musical. The archer looked to the men standing before us and shrugged. Then an old, white-haired man, at least as thin as the woman, elbowed his way to the front and rasped, "Welcome to our village. Is this the language you understand?"

"Yes," Gairen responded immediately, bringing smiles and nods from the other villagers standing before us. "We're in search of a king whom we believe to be to the northeast of your village somewhere."

"Well, you're welcome to rest here a bit," the old one said squeakily, "but we don't know anything about any people living northeast of here." He shrugged. "We never go anywhere." He paused, as if choosing words carefully. "What's that strange creature you've brought with you and why is it allowed to ride on a horse?" His eyes darted toward the little one, in case he hadn't been completely understood.

Aldern responded perhaps a little too quickly. "He's our friend, this expedition being as much for his benefit as our own. He rides because we ride."

"Thank you for your hospitality," interjected the duke hastily, throwing a cold glance in Aldern's direction. "Though I'd still like to speak with anyone in your village who may have even an idea or has heard even an ancient legend, anything at all concerning what we may encounter in our travels to the northeast."

87

The elder seemed perturbed and wrinkled his nose in disdain. "Oh, all right. There is the foolish one called Poontala, who wandered off that way once and has babbled ever since. Not a brain in his head has he, but the few visitors we get here always seem to find him entertaining."

The white-haired translator made gestures that clearly showed he thought we were either foolish or crazy, as he turned to his companions and relayed our conversation into their native speech. Toward the end, the others rolled their eyes and started shaking their heads, then shrugged and moved off. The old man turned back and mumbled, "Follow me."

We wound our way through a maze of small houses and worn paths, all roughly of the same shape, size, and description, finally arriving at one with a large stone propped against some weathered pieces of wood covering the entrance. Our guide hollered shrilly at a couple of young men a little ways off. They stopped what they were doing immediately to come and remove the stone covering the entrance of the house, then stood at either side in guard-like fashion.

The low doorway being cleared, our guide dropped to a squatting position in front it, calling something into the gloom inside of the small house. He turned and mumbled something to one of the young men, who then ran off and returned with a small torch. The old one stood again, then stooped and entered, gesturing for some of us to follow. I was curious and gently pushed my way in. Velarso, the duke, Gairen, the little one, and Sir Trendall entered also, while the rest of our company waited outside.

The inside of the house was plastered with a pale brown mud, the whole structure being somewhat circular, perhaps dome shaped. The torch was touched to a point in the center of the floor and a small fire sprang up, lighting the interior and creating wisps of foul-smelling smoke. There was a smaller doorway along a far wall through which the old man disappeared momentarily. He reappeared again accompanied by a fairly young man who had a wild look in his eyes.

"This," said the old man, "is Poontala. If you'd please just sit down somewhere, anywhere, we can begin. He says he's glad that you've come." The old one rolled his eyes again and shook his head slightly.

The duke turned from Poontala to the old man. "Tell him--"

"I can answer for myself," Poontala said.

Sir Trendall's eyebrows shot up.

"We are traveling toward the northeast, in search of a king," Gairen said.

"The king of the Castle Mirus, King Treston? Yes, he's there, but the foolish people of this village don't believe in anything beyond their own immediate sight or experience."

The three leaders of our group were clearly dumbfounded. "So what can you tell us, that we may find him with minimal difficulty?" Gairen said, trying to hide his astonishment.

The young prisoner laughed loud and long, causing puzzled looks to pass between us.

"'With minimal difficulty' you say," Poontala smirked, but a severe look from Sir Trendall sobered him. "All right. The first part of the trip will bring you onto the eastern portion of the great plain. There's nothing there to harm or to help you. Then the air grows drier, the climate hotter. You begin to encounter desert cities with buildings the size of small mountains. The people you'll meet there are strange."

The knight sneered. "A fine thing for you to be saying."

The youth shrugged. "Maybe it's the place from which you came. They're all a bunch of snobs there, you know. Anyway, you pass through there and watch for the eastern forest, which isn't nearly as big as the western one, and there you find your royal highness."

"So how did a youth with such an impertinent attitude learn all these things?" the duke said demurely.

The youth leaned forward. "Enough of these questions, he whispered. "Are you going to bust me out of here or not? The duke's eyes shot open, not having even considered such a thing.

"We've been warned not to," Gairen answered for the duke.

The old man squinted and nodded slightly, his first action since the conversation began.

"What?" Poontala shrieked in anger. "I told you everything you wanted to know, didn't I?"

"That," said Gairen quietly, "is the real question."

Catching his drift, Sir Trendall added, "There's nothing you've left out, forgotten to mention?"

Poontala immediately grew quiet, gritted his teeth, and stormed back to the other room with only an angry groan instead of bidding us any farewell.

"Is he not a foolish one?" The elder villager chuckled. "He knows enough to be interesting but not enough to be helpful. I'd urge you to disregard what he's said, because I have my own reasons for believing that you won't find the land to the northeast to be as he has told you."

"So what will we find?" I said anxiously.

"You'll be fine," the old one responded quickly, closing his eyes and giving a placating nod with his head. "So don't trouble yourself with fears that have no substance." Opening his eyes, he added, "There are many things that it's best to learn for yourself."

"So why do you keep him locked up?" said Gairen as we all moved back outside.

"He has insufficient self-control," replied the white-haired man.

"Why not send him away, exile him to some other people with whom he'd be happier?" Sir Trendall suggested.

"Because," the old man said in a low voice, "it's not the way of my people to do so."

A long silence followed, as he and the knight stared into each other's flinty eyes.

The two young villagers finished resecuring the entrance, waved, and wandered off.

"We don't wish to offend in any way," Gairen said, trying to smooth things a bit, "but would request, if it should be convenient for you, some additional provisions for our quest: food, water, whatever you think we may need."

The old one brightened at this statement and tipped his head slightly. "If you'll wait on the edge of the meeting grounds in the center of town, even make your camp in the manner to which you're accustomed, if you like, I'll see what I can procure for you. I suspect my fellow townspeople will be generous, in that we're in the midst of celebrating the harvest." With that he turned and was gone.

"All fine and dandy, but just how do we get to these so-called 'meeting grounds'?" mumbled Roshto.

"I think I saw the place on the way here," said Drinlar, "at the end of one of the wider streets we crossed."

"Well, lead on," said Gairen.

The villagers had no horses, so it was an easy task to follow our tracks back to the wide street in question. Drinlar led the way from there into a surprisingly large open area, ringed with wooden posts that might have supported tents or nets, or perhaps a curtain of some kind. We moved out a short distance and began to set up camp, as the old one had suggested.

I heard a gasp right next to me. "Nifgon, look!"

I whirled to face the direction in which Nartok was pointing. Towering over the town, frighteningly unreal in some way, the smooth wall of the sandstone bluff was scarred with a deep and wide crack: the chasm of Taevius.

CHAPTER 15

My Continuing Memories:
A Night of Remembering, Pondering, and Waiting

A quiet night hung over our little camp. The villagers all stayed away, though we heard faint murmurs from time to time in the houses surrounding the open area where we were. The moon offered only the faintest light, so the crack in the bluff was nearly invisible. Still, it felt as if an ominous specter loomed over the camp. I stared into the darkness where the chasm lay hidden and felt as if I were confronted with the jaws of a dragon, waiting for the appropriate moment to devour me.

Ehrgsos stepped to my side and stared into the gloom also. "It's an eerie feeling, isn't it little one," he said, "but I'd wager you feel differently this time."

I glanced upward to read his thoughtful expression.

"It's a serious thing to face the phantoms of one's past," he said, "but a different matter altogether when one's approaching the conflict with the mentality of a warrior rather than of a victim." He turned his face to mine and spoke with confidence. "Go forth to conquer, my little friend. After years of preparation, the victory shall be yours."

I pondered his words when he'd moved away to warm himself by the fire again. It was true. I didn't feel afraid. Yet I was aware that I was facing some great challenge. What if I was not victorious? Would that make me less of a warrior and more of a victim?

Velarso appeared at my side, having seen but not heard my interaction with Ehrgsos. "Are you troubled, my friend?"

I didn't answer, still staring into the darkness.

He put his arm around my shoulders and my eyes turned to meet his. He smiled, drew me closer, and pulled his cloak over both our shoulders. "Let me tell you a story." He said. "Once upon a time, long ago and far away, a man had a small piece of ground in a rocky and somewhat mountainous land. He worked hard to feed his family with the things he planted and cultivated there and usually managed to harvest just enough each year, to survive and be healthy and strong. Then someone gave him a bull and a cow, in gratitude for the kind hospitality he'd shown them when they'd travelled near his house and been given shelter for the night. The cow provided a good supply of milk for the man's family, but the bull was high-spirited and difficult to control. A few months went by, and one night a thunderstorm appeared in the sky just before dusk. The animals grew more agitated with each flash of lightening and blast of thunder. Fearing they'd break out of their enclosure, the man ran out of the house to try to calm them, only to find they'd already gone. When the sun rose the next morning, he took a length of rope and set out to retrieve the animals, leaving his wife, two sons, and a daughter at home. While he was gone, however, the two animals came back because they were hungry and vegetation was sparse in that land. The two sons were outside mending the fences of the enclosure, the elder saw the bull approaching and ran for the house. The younger turned to see his escape cut off before he could do the same." Velarso fell silent and turned his gaze upward.

"Well, what happened?" I said, when it seemed he'd say no more.

"The younger boy took a long, thin branch lying nearby, marched right up to the bull, and whipped him across the nose. The bull jumped back in surprise. The young boy circled behind the bull, who was now obviously confused. Yelling and snapping the branch through the air, the boy stomped around. The bull side-stepped to get out of the way and soon found himself standing back inside the enclosure. The cow moved to stand by her mate and the little boy stood guard until his father got home.

I blinked my eyes in amazement. "And the father was very proud of his son's courage."

"No," Velarso said quickly. "He reprimanded him for acting so foolishly."

"But the cattle were returned to their enclosure and everyone was safe. What more did the man want?"

94

"He wanted his son to be just as wise as he was brave." A long silence followed. "You're being very brave, my little friend; remember to be wise also."

I found his narrative somewhat confusing, or rather, I wasn't sure exactly what Velarso was trying to tell me. "What are you saying? What have I said or done to give you the impression that I am being brave but not altogether wise?" I asked him.

"You have not given me the impression that you are not being altogether wise," Velarso corrected. "I am only concerned that wisdom is not forgotten during the days ahead. I expect them to be quite challenging. Perhaps you will understand better as the coming days unfold around us."

"But who's to say what's truly wise?" I replied. "If the boy knew the mannerisms of the bull, that he would respond with obedience to the boy's confidence, wasn't the action he took the wisest one?"

Velarso smiled sheepishly. "Yes. Part of wisdom is to recognize that it won't always be recognized as such, even by those whom we love. For your own survival and victory, you must always listen to your own heart. It may not speak loudly or clearly, but it will never lie."

"The little boy in the story was you."

"Yes, he was," Velarso tried to hide another grin. "My father taught me many things without realizing that he did, but he was unwilling to learn from me and thus the bull one day claimed my father's life. I was gone with my brother on some errand or other, otherwise I might've been able to intervene and save him." Velarso swallowed and his eyes grew wet for the briefest moment.

I snuggled closer to my friend's broad, muscled chest. "It's possible that I'll again confront my own father before this adventure is over." I sighed. "I don't know what I will say to him." I looked into Velarso's eyes again. "When that time comes," I said, "I hope that the words spoken will be the ones that need to be spoken."

We stared into the darkness for a while longer, the camp's fire at our backs, pondering a wealth of unknowns, tired but not sleepy. Eftral appeared on my right unexpectedly, stared into the darkness with us and then suggested a continuation of the narrative of my first escape from Taevius. I turned to see most of the rest of our company with their gaze fixed on us, waiting for a response. I looked to Velarso, who nodded, and we returned to the warmth of the fire.

I began where I'd left off, approaching a castle on a high ridge. "The hill dropped away sharply behind me, into the deep forest. Hours away was the ridge I'd traversed earlier, with the very first suggestions of dawn peeking over it. My feet ached more than I can say and I was exhausted. Wandering off the path a bit, I found a long-needled pine bush at the base of a larger tree and flopped to the ground in its moonshadow. In the village below I began to hear voices. Somewhere in the castle above me, a large dog barked."

"It seemed I only blinked my eyes and the rosy glow of dawn was far-advanced across the sky. When I blinked again, the sun was high over my head. My eyes shot open but I froze. The eyes staring back into mine belonged to the biggest dog I'd ever seen. His grey, wiry coat looked brushed and clean, but he wasn't growling, like the ill-tempered mongrels of Taevius always seemed to be. After what seemed like an eternity, an older man's voice called out some strange word and the hound looked away but declined to move from the place where he stood. There was a rustling in the bushes to my left and some more strange words. Barely daring to breathe, I stared at the dog. Then a man dressed in expensive-looking clothes, unlike any I'd ever seen, appeared at the dog's side and peered into my face. The dog seemed to relax. I did too, a little. The elderly gentleman said some words to me, but I could only reply with expressions of absolute bewilderment. Finally, he shrugged, pushed the dog away, and gestured for me to follow."

"He started back toward the path, then looked to see if I was coming. He seemed trustworthy. I got up and stumbled after him, throwing my brown cloak around me as soon as I got to the path. Past a drawbridge and a castle gate, the old man opened an imense door and led me through a labyrinth of corridors and stairways, stopping at last to knock at an average-sized but ornately carved chamber entrance. Some more strange words. It seemed an almost musical language but with the staccatoness of galloping horses hooves."

"The first man kindly ushered me into a room where several others stood around a lavishly decorated chair. All were staring at me. Finally, one approached and lifted my cloak away. The room was instantly absolutely silent. Another of the men nodded and the rest began to whisper among themselves. A young boy and the man who'd brought me there took my hands and led me out, bringing my brown wrap."

"It seemed we climbed an endless chain of stairs to a small room with three windows twice the width of my hand and just low enough for me to see out. They gestured for me to go inside and with smiles and nods made an unhurried exit. I was alone, but felt strangely content."

"The view through the windows was grand indeed. I must've been in one of the highest towers of the fortress. Below me, green and golden fields and forests stretched from horizon to horizon. It was all so beautiful. People scurried about in the village below like tiny insects, their voices barely audible to me and their speech completely unintelligible anyway. The room held a rough-hewn bed made from thick tree branches, a small stool of similar construction, and a couple of old woven blankets, but there was also a small door opposite the bed. I hadn't notice it when I first came in. Evidently no one had used this door in quite some time, but it finally gave way and swung inward on ancient leather hinges. Outside I found a narrow balcony running all the way around the tower. The height almost made me dizzy, but the air smelled so sweet and the sparrows flitting to and fro seemed particularly joyous. This was the world the old man in the cave had been talking about. It was incredible."

It seemed time to stop for the night, judging by the sleepy expressions on my friends' faces and my own tired eyelids as well. The specter of Taevius's chasm still loomed in the darkness around our small camp, but we'd sleep well anyway, knowing that future battles had no power to harm us until their appointed day and hour had come. I looked into the darkness toward Taevius one more time as I lay down to sleep, knowing that the battles most certainly would come. Hopefully I would be ready. Significant battles, it seems to me, first seem to take a long time, then seem to have arrived too soon, then seem to last an eternity, and ultimately immediately fade into a sort of timelessness, as if they occurred both yesterday and also long ago. It would have been helpful, in any case, to know a little more clearly just what it was, for which I was fighting.

CHAPTER 16

Ahdrynne's Chapter

A sudden clanging shot through our sleeping heads. Nartok understood first. The village was in an uproar because an early-morning stroll by one of the local citizens had betrayed the presence of Taevians climbing through the crack in the bluff. Evidently having trekked the length of the chasm, they were swarming toward the town with murderous knives drawn. Panic and pandemonium swept through the streets ahead of them.

"Ahdrynne," Gairen called to me. "What's going on?"

"Taevians, sir. Hundreds of them," I replied.

"Taevians?" the duke shouted in disbelief. "Here?"

The old villager appeared. "So will you run or will you help us?" he said angrily. "Surely it's you who've brought this trouble to my people."

Sir Trendall pushed his way to the front. "What defenses do you have? What actions are being taken?"

"None. We have neither weapons nor means of escape. Until now, we've never needed such things," the elder replied hotly.

The knight looked around quickly, in desperate frustration. "Tell everyone to run. They shouldn't try to hide because every structure will be torn down before these wicked Taevians leave. Fighting is senseless since we're hopelessly outnumbered."

The old one gritted his teeth and shook his head slowly. "No. This is our home. We'll drive them out or we'll die. We don't wish to have any other life than what we've known."

Sir Trendall put his hand to his head and turned away quickly, pacing, then turned and said vehemently, "Resistance is suicide." Seeing the man unmoved, he growled fiercely in frustration. "I'll stay for the sake of my own honor. I can't ask any other to give up his life for your refusal to leave this place."

The man turned and strode away angrily. The knight spun about and began barking out orders to our company. "Nartok,

99

Drinlar, and Verbont, get the horses loaded and ready to go with all the provisions you can find. Whoever wants to leave can leave; I'll stay to fight as long as I can."

The duke was already scrambling to his horse, not even looking back to concern himself with the safety of the others.

Turning to Velarso and I, Sir Trendall paused briefly, then said more calmly, "You two will escort the little one safely out of harm's reach. Go and may all that's good protect you." The knight turned away. "Aldern and Esstrol, start stringing rope and anything else you can find between those poles to form a barricade, behind which the archer could be our greatest asset, if he wants to stay, that is." Sir Trendall turned to Gairen with the question posed in a facial expression.

"I'll stay," the archer said resolutely, readying his quiver and bow.

I brought three saddled horses but Velarso seemed reluctant to run from battle. Sir Trendall turned to him again. "If our little friend doesn't safely reach the king of Castle Mirus, wherever he may be, then this entire expedition will today be wiped from history and all of Nypothnia may be doomed for centuries to come. Our hope against the Taevians lies with the wizard-king. Find him or all is lost."

Velarso nodded quickly, staring at the ground.

"We must hurry," I reminded him, climbing onto my own horse. With a quick turn, his strong hands lifted the little one onto the second horse. For a second they stared into each others' eyes. Then Velarso leapt to his own horse and took the lead as we raced away through the city's narrow, winding streets. A Taevian soldier burst into our path from a cross-street. With an angry battle cry, Velarso drove his horse right over the man. A couple more Taevians appeared, but we were moving too fast for them to even attempt to stop us. In moments, the last house of the village was behind us.

The wind whipped at our clothing. The little one buried his face in the mane of his deep-brown steed and hung on. Velarso was still leading the way, riding fast but with his face turned toward the village behind us. Then he began to rein in his horse.

We stopped and looked back. The village was quite distant now. Smoke was rising from the area nearest to the crack in the bluff.

"I have to go back. Can you see our little friend safely to the wizard-king by yourself?" Velarso asked me.

I didn't know what to say. I felt the loss of friends, but knew there was nothing I could offer to help them. "If you must go back, then I won't hinder you. But isn't it better to avenge our comrades by completing the original mission, than to die with them?"

The silence between us was heavy indeed. Finally he swallowed and whispered, "There shall be a day of justice and judgment for the evil that's been done, and I'll be there." He put his hand to his forehead for a moment, then wiped his eyes quickly before turning to look upon the village one more time. Our little friend looked from one of us to the other with a questioning gaze, so I nodded and forced a smile to him, wanting the little one to understand that everything would be okay.

We turned our horses from the village again, glancing back frequently as we moved away. We let the horses walk for a while, and soon the village faded from view. Only the smoke rising high over the bay betrayed its location.

The sun was high and hot above us and our shadows small beneath us when the sandstone bluffs to our left gave way to gently rolling hills. We turned our horses inland, away from the Bay of Brendwolt. As the land flattened out still more, we urged our horses to canter and evening found us on a pleasant, grassy plain. We'd travelled as close to true northeast as we could. In the distance, the land seemed to rise into hills and perhaps even mountains more or less covered with trees.

With a few provisions from our saddlebags, a small supper and a warm fire were soon managed. Having eaten, we all sat together with one heavy cloak around our shoulders, staring at the dancing flames of our dwindling campfire.

Velarso spoke for the first time since that morning. "Esstrol told me once of a young girl waiting for him in the land of Phrynondi. She wanted him to live there with her, hunting the exotic lehrnoto that live in the swamps. Their meat is considered a delicacy in that part of Nypothnia. They would've made a good living. Smoked lehrnoto isn't cheap."

"What's lehrnoto?" the little one asked.

"The lehrnoto is a secretive animal," I answered, "best hunted at dawn, when its pale, oily skin is easily seen in the dark mud of the swamps. That's the only time it comes up for air. The rest of the time it stays far below the surface, feeding on certain roots. I've never actually seen one myself, but Esstrol said that they're long tubular creatures, about as long as a man's arm and about as big around. They have eight to ten stubby little limbs with large webbed paddles so that they can resubmerge themselves into the mud very quickly if they need to. But they're also blind and deaf. They sense everything through their skin. Not much to look at, but very tasty, I'm told."

"I'll take your word for it," our little friend mumbled, with a sour expression and a brief shudder. Velarso laughed a little at the reaction and I smiled, happy to hear the sound of laughter again in our camp.

We were almost asleep and fire was low, when a sudden stirring of the wind jerked us all awake again. Something felt eerie, but also familiar. Then, there she was again: Masra.

She looked a little older than before and bore a somber expression. "Greetings, friends," she whispered, almost sadly.

"You come and go like the wind," Velarso growled softly. "You seem to have powers and abilities that I couldn't begin to explain, yet you do nothing to help when our entire company is in grave danger. Our success is needed by yourself equally as much as by everyone else."

"Yes," Masra said softly.

Velarso's anger was growing. "So where were you?

"I did what I could and wanted you to know, so that you may receive at least some encouragement for the days ahead."

Velarso started to speak again, but I put my hand on his arm to hold his words a moment. "So what happened?"

"I couldn't save all," she said, "but Ehrgsos and Nartok are following your trail with two horses loaded with provisions. Drinlar, Riomar, and Roshto escaped toward the west and will have a difficult time rejoining you, if they decide to try. Gairen fared well enough to do what good he could before escaping into the sea. He may join you yet. I've sent a great sea creature to ferry him away to a safe inlet somewhere. The duke escaped by means of his cowardice, but his horse has gone lame in a desolate place and he may not survive."

"I may have a hard time feeling sorry for him," Velarso said, uncharacteristically cynical.

Masra forced a brief smile. "Aldern was seriously injured, but survived by feigning death. He was able to escape because the Taevians returned to the chasm when they felt that enough provisions and valuables had been stripped from the victims. His injuries won't take his life, but he's returning to the west and will need time to recover." With a deep and grievous sigh, Masra continued. "Eftral, Nifgon, and Verbont fell in battle. They fought bravely and nobly but it was a battle for honor, not for victory."

"I suspected as much," I sighed.

"My comrade, Esstrol?" Velarso pressed.

Masra shook her head slowly. "Esstrol engaged the high priest of Taevius in personal combat. The spirit-leader employed much trickery, yet Esstrol prevailed. Then came the priest's brother and ran his long sword all the way through Esstrol from behind, but your comrade spun around so swiftly that the grip slipped from the brother's hand and the point of his own sword thus sliced him fatally across the stomach. The priest leapt forward to strike again but Esstrol seized his shoulders and drew him into an embrace of death on his brother's long sword. Bards will sing of his valour for generations to come."

Velarso was silent. His shoulders trembled, his face grew wet, and his fists shook in anger and grief. I put one hand on his shoulder and with the other took the hand of the little one, drawing the three of us together into a collective embrace.

I turned once more to Masra, "Leave us alone to grieve. If you have more to say, it must wait. Thank you for what aid you were able to supply."

She nodded and with a gentle surge in the wind was swept from our view.

When the dawn kissed the land again, I jumped to my feet in alarm. Velarso was nowhere to be seen, though our little companion was only beginning to awake, judging by the slight movements under his blanket.

Relief came a moment later, however, when Velarso appeared a short distance away, walking quietly through medium-tall grass. He seemed more at ease, smiling as he drew closer. "I just needed to be alone a while, to sort some things out."

I nodded and smiled. The heaviest of the grief had perhaps passed, for Velarso at least.

There was still no sign of Nartok and Ehrgsos with the two supply horses. We loaded our horses again and started onward at a moderately slow pace, to allow them to catch up with us more easily. It was a pleasant day of riding across vast plains, the grass becoming ever taller until only ourselves and our horses' heads could be seen. Toward evening, we chose a campsite on a low ridge about halfway between our last campsite and the mountains in the distance. After quite a bit of digging and chopping with our swords, we managed a safe spot for a campfire and settled in for the night.

Velarso was tired and drifted off to sleep earlier than usual, leaving our little friend and I to stare into dancing flames and reflect on the events of the last few days.

"How are you, really?" I asked my small companion.

"With each face that appears to me in the flames of the small fire--Eftral, Nifgon, Verbont, Esstrol, Sir Trendall--a lump in my throat grows larger and harder to swallow," he answered. "Oh, Adrynne..." He began to cry and I quickly held out my hand to invite an embrace. The little, young man fell against my chest and I wrapped my arms around him as he trembled and softly sobbed his losses into my shirt.

Velarso jerked awake, saw what was happening and gestured to me. I carried our little friend to him, laying our small companion in the strong arms of my fellow guard, then turned away to put more wood on the fire. I spread another thick blanket on the ground next to my two friends and wrapped yet another one across my shoulders. Then I lay down next to them

104

and spread the last blanket across all three of us, the little one thus kept warm by our bodies on each side of him.

I awoke the next morning to see the little one's head resting on Velarso's chest, and felt the reassuring touch of his large hands upon my own chest. Then, in the distance, I heard a voice. I looked around quickly, then jumped up without fully waking my companions.

Velarso's head rested on a pile of tall grasses we'd cut when clearing the campsite, his eyes still closed in sleep. I said his name quietly, then a little louder. Finally he stirred, opened his eyes, then jumped up so quickly that he almost knocked me over. His hand steadied me a for a split-second, then he was gone, sprinting off through the tall grass a fast as he could.

Nartok and Ehrgsos were racing for our little camp, shouting and waving their arms in celebration. In moments the five of us were gathered at our encampment and it seemed the smiles and hugs and shouts of joy would never end. We shared a joyous breakfast together while they told the tale of their escape from the battle. Last came the difficult task of relaying what Masra had told us of the fates of our friends. A few more tears were shed. Then it was time to move on, to remember that our goal wasn't yet accomplished, that Nypothnia wasn't yet safe.

We got underway quickly, the morning being perhaps half gone. The tall grass thinned out into a more arid plain. Spirits were high as we cantered along, drawing near to the first trees in the shadow of the mountains in late afternoon. When we camped for the night, the trees weren't quite so dense as a forest, but firewood was abundant and the wind soared high overhead where the trees couldn't reach.

But then the wind swept down through the trees and my gaze turned to Velarso, who responded with a knowing nod of his head. Masra had returned to deliver the rest of her message. Nartok took a seat on a small boulder near the fire as she stepped into the firelight from the west side of our camp.

"It's been a difficult time for all of us," she began, "but if I may offer some encouragement, the king isn't far away. I'm unable to discern exactly where, but I sense that he's very near."

"I am puzzled as to the source and accuracy of your perceptions," Velarso said, a trifle skeptical, "but do tell us whatever you can."

Masra hesitated, evidently unsure of what to say next. "I have nothing else to say. I've been working very hard at it, but can't come up with any more answers for you. Please don't be discouraged, because you're very close." She stopped and then added lamely, "I wish I could help more." Her shoulders sank in discouragement and she sighed deeply. "I'll leave you to yourselves." Then she was gone.

"Did she appear older or younger?" I asked. Then, without waiting for any answer, added, "Perhaps her difficulties in perception are related to the aging of her body. I think she needs to rejoin the king very soon."

"If that's the source of her problems," said Ehrgsos, "just think of what the king must be experiencing."

Nartok nodded and rose from the boulder he sat on. "Tomorrow we'll survey the surrounding mountains to determine where a refuge of some kind might be built or located."

I leaned against Velarso's shoulder and whispered, "Do you think we'll find the king tomorrow?"

Velarso's gaze met mine a moment, then he quietly responded, "The king is hiding from his enemies. He may not be able to do so without also hiding from his friends.

CHAPTER 17

My Continuing Memories:
Accomplishment and Closure

My four friends were up early.

"Good morning, little friend." Velarso gently woke me and gestured to a small assortment of fruit, bread, and warm roasted meat near the fire.

Evidently the others had eaten already and were anxious to get on with the search. I wiped the sleep from my eyes and stumbled toward the fire, trying to wake up. Ehrgsos glanced my way and chuckled. Ahdrynne's hand caught me as I stumbled, steadied my shoulder, and guided me to sit on a large rock near the collection of burning branches, twigs, and grass. I threw him the comical smile of someone who's still half asleep as a thank you. He smiled back and tousled my hair playfully, then moved off to help with the horses.

Nartok was already on his horse, suggesting that we maintain our present encampment and search in pairs.

"And what of our little friend?" said Velarso.

"He may be the third to whichever pair he wishes," Nartok replied. "In that this is unfamiliar land for all of us, I don't think it wise for anyone to be alone."

The others nodded agreement and turned for my decision. I gestured a question, since my mouth was filled with a big bite of apple.

Ahdrynne nodded. "The pairings will be Nartok and Ehrgsos and Velarso and myself?"

Again, there was immediate agreement. I thought a moment and decided that the first day I'd go with Ahdrynne and Velarso and that if our search proved unfruitful, I'd join Nartok and Ehrgsos on the morrow. The arrangements being made, our camp was quickly brought to order and all provisions carefully camouflaged and secured a few paces away, in case an unknown person or animal happened by. Nartok and Ehrgsos were gone just moments later, heading slightly to the northeast. We left soon after, bending more to the southeast. The horses were well-rested, the sun was shining, and our spirits were high.

The ground quickly grew steeper beneath us, urging us toward a narrow valley where a small stream trickled out, evidently from some source higher in the mountains. We chose to follow the stream, reasoning that the king would need a supply of water no matter where he was. The going was much easier for us for a while. Then the soil changed to a strange mixture of sand, black dirt, and rock, such that our mounts soon could go no faster than a brisk walk. It was pretty--the saplings, wild flowers, and general topography, accompanied by the musical gurgling of the brook--but there was also a strange empty feeling, as if people had never lived here before. Yet as I listened and looked, I decided it wasn't so much a feeling of emptiness as of solitude and harmony. The absence of people provided for an absence of the emotional and spiritual turbulence that most people inevitably bring with them.

Ahdrynne gently whispered to remain quiet and pointed to the right with a slight smile. We turned quickly to see a dozen or so large deer bounding away through the brush that covered the lower part of the mountains. Gazing higher up, I saw how the trees reached for the sky but stopped at a certain point and were replaced by brush, which gave way still higher up to a smooth, green carpet. Even this couldn't reach the humbling height of the rocky grey summits. It was the first time that I'd felt both very small and simultaneously also both surrounded and filled with a sense of majesty--a sort of inner greatness that extended outwards through all things, somehow connecting me with all things.

All through the morning, we wound our way higher and farther, the air growing slightly colder. Ahdrynne commented that perhaps this was where the spirit of winter lived during those times of the year when it wasn't permitted to envelop the land. Velarso was deep in thought, scanning the woods around us intensely. He offered no response. I smiled and nodded to Ahdrynne.

Then we came upon a small lake, evidently the source of the brook, its surface so smooth as to mirror the loftiness of the mountain peak that lay directly ahead. We dismounted and took in the beauty of the place for a few moments.

Velarso sighed deeply, interrupting the thoughtful moment. "Either we are searching in the wrong direction, or we are searching in the wrong manner," he said at last.

Ahdrynne sighed also, then suggested, "Let's have a little something to eat and start back down. Perhaps there are things visible from above that aren't visible from below. We may have passed within a few feet of something significant and not even known it."

"If that's truly the case," said Velarso, "then the best vantage point for our search is the summit that still lies beyond us."

Ahdrynne grew more thoughtful. "That's true, I suppose, but I have no experience in climbing mountains. Any man can see that the terrain only grows more steep. We'd have to split up and someone stay with the horses."

In the long, pondering silence that followed, I stared at the peak, as if trying to map its face with routes of ascent. All possibilities looked equally difficult to me from where we now stood, yet something told me that I needed to stand on that summit, that the climb was absolutely essential in some way.

"Little friend," said Ahdrynne, interrupting my thoughts. Evidently he'd called several times without getting a response. "We've decided to return to our camp to discuss the matter with our comrades. Perhaps we'll make an ascent on the morrow with all of us working together."

"We must get to the top of that peak," I said, with confidence coming from an unknown source. "We must at least try--today." Expressions of disbelief stared back at me. "Let's at least go until we know we can go no farther." They were unpersuaded. "I don't know how, but somehow I do know that I must get to the top of this mountain."

Speechless, they still stared, first at each other, then at me. Finally, Ahdrynne shrugged.

Velarso cleared his throat softly. "We'll see what can be done."

He guided his horse to lead the way around the small lake toward the summit ahead. I couldn't explain the excited anticipation I began to feel. The far side of the lake, however, brought another sigh of frustration from each of my friends. The terrain suddenly became so rocky that it was obvious the horses could go no further. A bit of deliberation preceded the decision that Velarso and I would continue upward and that Ahdrynne would tend to the horses there by the lake. We'd be able to see him throughout most of the remaining ascent.

The field of boulders proved more difficult and exhausting than I'd imagined. For a while it seemed I was always out of breath, but Velarso was having difficulty too. Puzzled and worried looks passed between us. Quite a while had passed since we'd left Ahdrynne by the lake. The summit looked so close each time I glanced up, but seemed to recede from us with each step. The wind grew stronger too, sometimes throwing our weary bodies off balance as we climbed over boulders and rocks of diverse sizes and shapes.

Velarso's face grew unusually pale and he stopped and called to me at last, taking deep gasping breaths between each few words. "Surely the...air...in this place...is bewitched...in some way. Be careful that...it does not overcome you...I must rest here...Go on...I'll be able...to see you and...come to your aid...if you..."

I was breathing hard too, but understood and waved to him to be silent. Something about the two of us staggering along always out of breath struck me as being very funny, but he seemed very concerned, so I refrained from joking about our situation. Nodding and gesturing agreement, I struggled onward.

At last, I was nearly to the top. I looked back to Velarso--a tiny spot in the expanse of grey stone around him--and he waved to me. I wrapped my long fingers over the last grey ledge and pulled myself up. It was a long moment before I stopped breathing hard and slowly stood up to survey the world around me, around this mountaintop.

Never had I been so filled with awe. A few scattered clouds floated in the bluest sky I'd ever seen, some higher and some lower that the summit on which I stood. The land stretched out for incomprehensible distances in all directions. To the east were peaks even grander and higher than this one. Some wore glistening white crowns. To the north and to the south, the mountains extended like soldiers marching in formation, a vast green and brown plain lying before them to the west. I sat in silent prayer for a while, then offered a poem the silence had created within me.

> "In sacred places of vaulted earth,
> in dancing winds with thundering mirth,
> in ageless stones, the mountain's wings,
> the soul of life in silence sings.
> In candle's flame and blooming flower,
> I feel I'm followed, hour by hour,
> by beauty great and deep and wise
> and the power of love begins to rise.
> I launch my ears toward every word,
> that cries of pain and joy be heard,
> in winter's cold and summer's rain,
> and a greater me, at last reclaim."

"How beautiful," Velarso said, suddenly right behind me. "Is that something you read someplace and committed to memory?"

"Well, actually," I looked away, a tiny bit embarrassed at having been overheard, "it's just something I made up."

"I'm impressed," my friend responded, "Perhaps you have an undiscovered talent for composing words which touch the soul. So, other than that, what is it that keeps my friend so long on the mountaintop?" he said when almost by my side.

"Look around at my inspiration," I responded.

He gazed around us, quickly displaying the same look of awe as I must've had. Then I remembered our initial intention that brought us to this place, and began to survey the lands below for any signs of a structure or the presence of people other than ourselves.

"Something," Velarso said, still transfixed by the natural wonder, "something that touches your soul. Something beautiful."

His smile broadened as the wind tousled his hair, as if he were hearing some new music also. The sun cast a healthy glow over his face. I smiled; he seemed even more ruggedly beautiful and handsome. He turned and swept me off of my feet in a great bear-hug. So he felt it too, I concluded to myself, that wonderful feeling of self-worth and accomplishment, knowing that he and I and everyone had a special place in the great and beautiful world in which we lived.

At last we sat down to consider the land below together, but we failed to locate anything unusual that could indicate the presence of the wizard-king. So we made as many mental notes as we could and stood to rejoin our comrade at the lake. It certainly didn't take as long to get down as it had to come up.

"What did you see?" Ahdrynne asked excitedly, when we were barely within hearing.

The sun was headed for its nightly resting place so we signaled for him to wait until we were on our way back to the encampment below. We'd have to hurry somewhat if we were to escape having to pick our way back slowly in the dark.

"It's not so much what we saw as what we felt," Velarso said. "But we were unable to locate anything specific."

"We took note of anything that seemed even the least bit unusual," I added, "so that we can discuss everything with Nartok and Ehrgsos, but saw nothing that indicates the wizard-king's presence." I paused, then asked, "Did anything happen at the lake while we were gone?"

Ahdrynne shook his head. "Not a solitary thing. I did a bunch of thinking, trying, as you said, to piece things together and also to speculate as to just where the wizard-king might try to hide, but I didn't come up with anything."

We rode along in silence. We finally reached the camp just as the last orange sun-glow disappeared from the grasslands to the west. Nartok already had a fire going. Ehrgsos was preparing the evening meal. They looked up with hopeful eyes when we approached, but Ahdrynne answered with a quick

112

shake of his head. We secured the horses and gathered around the fire just as Ehrgsos began dividing up the small feast among us.

"So what did we all see today?" Velarso began. "Anything at all may be a clue."

"Neither Nartok nor I found even the slightest evidence of human life anywhere," Ehrgsos reported. "But we stayed mostly at the bottom of the mountains, looking for caves or camouflaged shelters where trees and underbrush were thickest."

Nartok slowly shook his head, obviously disappointed.

"Velarso and our little friend went all the way to a summit," said Ahdrynne, "thinking that something could be detected from there."

"But let's consider what you did see," said Nartok. "Can you describe the lay of the land?"

"To the west of us is a great, rolling plain," Velarso began, "and to the east are rows and rows of mountains with occasional lower valleys and canyons. If the king has retreated farther to the east, into the less accessible mountain ranges, it will be a long and difficult task to reach him."

"Perhaps he hasn't hidden himself so far to the east," I countered hopefully. "We inspected each valley and chasm as carefully as possible, from our vantage point, but a closer inspection could reveal all sorts of things, which would be invisible at any distance."

"With the abilities this king reportedly has," Nartok said sadly, "it seems likely that he'd make himself less accessible."

Quiet discouragement began to settle over the camp.

"Then tomorrow we'll move the camp into the mountains," I said confidently, trying to lift my friends' spirits. They looked at me with blank expressions, then to each other, finally giving forced smiles and approving nods.

"Well," said Ehrgsos lightly, "then there's nothing more to be decided tonight. So, how about continuing the tale of your first escape from Taevius, my little friend? I believe your last news was of a room in a castle tower. Were you a guest or a prisoner?"

I fidgeted a second or two at the sudden change of focus, but cheerfully consented. "Probably not a prisoner, at least initially, but I'd also hesitate to say that I was a guest. No one came to see me for several weeks, except for a young boy named Carlin who brought me food and water from time to time. He seemed nice, but had evidently been told of my difficulties with the language of the land and began on the fourth day to teach me various words. It became a sort of game. If I'd been taught the particular word for the food he brought, I was required to guess it by name before he'd bring it into the room for me to eat. He was a good teacher, so I usually didn't have too much trouble. My meals were usually vegetables, fruits, and a bit of fowl or hare. After nearly two months we conversed almost freely, though there were still a great many things I didn't understand. My room might've seemed like a prison cell, except for Carlin's friendship and our occasional forays around the castle grounds--though I wasn't permitted to do so without him present. He taught me a curious game played with very small, round stones in a circle drawn in the dust on the floor. We didn't play that one too much, however, because I had difficulty manipulating such small objects with my oversized fingers. Often we'd stare out the window together, wondering out loud about the world we could see below."

"'Who are you anyway?' Carlin asked me one day. 'The king and his advisors do a great deal of talking and debating about you.'"

"'What do they say?' I responded. He was very quiet for a moment. I followed his gaze and realized he was just lost in thought, staring off into space. 'I'm sorry. Perhaps I shouldn't have asked.' I sat down onto the bed. Carlin remained at the window."

"Finally, without looking away from the window and in little more than a whisper, he said, 'They are afraid; not so much of you specifically, as of something they associate with you, perhaps something you remind them of.'"

"I trusted Carlin, so I spoke out boldly, though I kept my gaze on the floor. 'Does the name Taevius mean anything to them?'"

114

"Carlin whirled around with wide, frightened eyes. 'It's true then?'"

"'It's true that I fled from that awful city. Even there I was completely out of place. Nothing about myself makes sense to me. Do you hate me for something I can't change, or can I still call you my friend?' I asked."

"He rushed to the door, perhaps angry, perhaps afraid. 'Carlin, please at least bring me word of what is to become of me,' I said."

"He paused. 'Just leave as soon as you can,' he said, and he was gone."

"I felt deserted and imprisoned. I crawled to the balcony's door with my brown cloak and opened it. Outside the sun was setting, surrounded by great clouds of pink and orange and gold. I pulled the cloak about me and sank to the floor of the balcony, my back against the tower wall. When I closed my eyes, the old man from the cave appeared before me and the strange melody seemed to flow from out of nowhere again."

"A blast of cold wind told me I'd dozed off. The night was darker than I'd ever seen it and a storm was rolling in. Raindrops beat down big and heavy and I pulled myself deeper into the folds of the cloak."

"I thought I heard a voice over the roaring of the wind. The storm ceased abruptly and the moon came out and lit up the night. I wished for the wings of a bird to fly away, or for some sort of magic with which to escape."

"A voice behind me said, 'I came to give you this.' I turned around in surprise. Carlin held out an enormous armload of rope. 'I don't know whether it's long enough or not. Take it and get out of here.' He dumped the rope into my arms and started to duck back through the small door into the tower, but stopped a moment to look at me and said, 'Be careful out there, okay?' Then he was gone again."

"I tied the rope to the bed and threw the rest over the balcony railing through one of the windows. I couldn't see the bottom end of the rope, but had to believe that it was long enough. I couldn't stop thinking of Carlin as I made my escape. Perhaps friendship works its own kind of magic in all places and times, if we allow it to."

"In any case, the rope was kind of thin and hard for my long fingers to grip, but plenty strong. The height was dizzying even in the dark and I had no idea how far down I was about to climb or how long it would take to do so. Eventually, however, some branches brushed my legs and I found myself slipping down a wet embankment outside of the castle walls, using the tail end of the rope to keep from crashing into the surrounding bushes and vines."

"I floundered through the tangle of vegetation, eventually reaching the less troublesome underbrush of the forest around the town. It was still dark, so I chose the first path I came to and went as fast as I could, keeping the castle behind me. I passed a clearing from where I could see the castle silhouetted against the first light of dawn. To my left, a few candles betrayed the existence of the village. The whole panorama was beautiful in a rustic sort of way. It seemed a nice way to remember this place, and to remember Carlin. For days afterward I'd picture him in my mind, standing on the high balcony of that tower, gazing into the distance and perhaps thinking of me. At least I hoped he'd think of me, that maybe I was still considered his friend somehow. He was certainly a good friend to me."

"My journeys took me through many villages and through many people's lives: Brenwill the carpenter, Relden the baker, the alchemist, Jonathon Ellick the troubadour, Brother Benedict the friar, and so many others. It seems there's no end to the telling of a life, so perhaps, concerning my first escape from Taevius, we should call this the end."

It had grown late all too quickly. Nartok stirred the fire to life to discourage the cold night air, and we gathered our blankets about us for a good night's rest. The morning would find us embarking on the next stage of our journey. I was tired, but I also felt restless, as if another chapter in my life was drawing toward an end, leaving me to begin something else. I gazed one last time at the peaceful sleeping faces of my friends and felt an immense love for each of them, especially for

Velarso. Then I closed my eyes to sleep, to dream, and to awake to whatever the new day would bring.

CHAPTER 18

Ehrgsos's Chapter

Nartok and Ahdrynne were getting onto their horses when I woke. Velarso was rushing about the camp, frantically burying the coals, rolling up blankets, and tying bundles onto the packhorses so quickly that his fingers were a blur.

"Good morning, Ehrgsos," Nartok called. "It's nice to see that you're finally awake." What was the meaning of his sarcasm, I wondered.

I peered about through still sleepy eyes, finally interrupting Velarso. "Forgive my ignorance, but what's going on?"

"Our little friend is gone," he said quickly, his speech quiet and staccato. "I fear his life is again in danger and our negligence is entirely to blame." With a gesture of great anxiety, he added, "Someone should've been standing guard."

"I understood that Nartok was a very light sleeper," I replied. "And we did arrange ourselves around the little one, after all, so either he or his abductor would've had to climb over us in order for him to leave our camp. Has anyone found any signs of struggle, any evidence of an intruder," I said, standing, "anything to indicate the presence of unfriendly beasts?" The last was something I know we didn't even want to consider, but the question needed to be asked.

Ahdrynne and Nartok began circling the camp.

Velarso remained agitated, still searching the immediate campsite. "His horse is still here, so whoever..."

"Or whatever," I interjected, drawing a short and unpleasant stare.

"Whoever is responsible," Velarso repeated, "was only interested in our small companion. Neither supplies nor horses nor anything else in the entire camp have been touched."

The pounding of hooves cut short our grim speculations. Nartok and Ahdrynne were racing toward the camp at a full gallop.

119

"There are signs of someone walking away from our camp on the steeper ground to the south, where the soil is somewhat more loose," Ahdrynne reported.

"But only one set of footprints," added Nartok.

"So why are we waiting?" Velarso snapped. "The packhorses are loaded, the fire is out. We know neither how far he's been taken nor what may be done to him if we delay a moment longer."

"Velarso," I interrupted, "Please," I paused, modelling calmness toward him, "please calm down. Okay? This journey has already had more than its share of unusual events. The chances that something bad has happened to him are no greater than the chances that something good has happened, which we do not at this point understand." I grabbed his shoulder and looked into his eyes for a moment. "Okay?" Velarso stared back at me, starting to calm down. "Okay?" I said again.

He closed his eyes, took a deep breath, exhaled, and opened his eyes again. "Okay."

"Let's hope that all's well," Nartok said calmly, "but nevertheless waste no time in searching for him." We set out immediately, moving as quickly as we could without losing sight of the trail.

The sun was high in the sky when the trail grew fainter and turned directly toward the mountains. Trees thinned out and bushes and vines became more dense, making the trail harder to track.

Velarso nodded toward a glimmer in the sun--water. "That narrow valley."

But he was interrupted by half a dozen horsemen suddenly pouring out of the exact place to which he'd pointed. We'd obviously been seen.

"To the trees, to the trees." Ahdrynne shouted, as his horse reared and whirled to retreat. We turned just as quickly and followed his lead, plunging into the underbrush of the most densely wooded spot around, though even that offered little cover. Velarso reined in first, turning his horse and raising his sword, ready to fight. He glanced to us, ready to charge.

120

"Wait." I raised my hand toward the others, while staring at the horsemen distantly opposite from us, puzzled. "They don't follow but merely stand all in a row."

"Why would they wait?" Ahdrynne asked cautiously.

"They don't seem particularly interested in attacking," whispered Nartok.

"Look," I said, "a single rider is breaking off from the others, approaching at a brisk trot." I stared intently at the approaching figure for a long moment, doing some mental calculations of my own. "I'm going out to meet him."

Nervous looks passed between the others, but before any could protest I was off. I cantered slowly to an open area an arrow's flight from my three companions and slowed to a walk, stopping when the other came within the sound of my voice.

"You're the companions of a strange, misshapen creature?" the unfamiliar soldier called to me.

"Identify yourself," I shouted back.

He seemed irritated. "We're the servants of a king."

Hope rose in me. "The king of Castle Mirus, King Treston, the king who was unable to withstand the Taevians and fled, the king who was engaged to marry a woman named Masra?"

The soldier jerked his mounts reigns nervously, causing the horse to sidestep for a moment. "What do you wish with such a king?"

"We wish to assist him in the final defeat of the Taevians and request his aid on behalf of our little friend, whom I believe you refer to disrespectfully as a 'misshapen creature.'" The soldier paused, so I added, "If you have harmed him in any way, rest assured that you'll pay with your life."

He stuttered briefly before answering, "He's fine. He's absolutely fine. No harm has come to him and none shall. Wait where you are and I'll return shortly."

He wheeled his horse and was gone at a fairly brisk canter. His fellow guards gathered closely around when he reached them, giving strong reactions to each part of his report. I was unable to hear their words, but understood them to be debating something. Finally reaching a consensus, he with whom I'd spoken came back toward me at a brisk canter again, his

121

compatriots following at a walk. I glanced behind me, suddenly a little anxious, and noticed my three comrades edging out of the woods at a brisk trot as well.

This time the spokesman came much closer. I smiled respectfully and noticed that he was much younger than he sounded or looked from a distance. He returned a nervous smile while we waited, his horse shifting from foot to foot as if equally nervous. When the five unfamiliar soldiers were close enough behind him to overhear, and my friends were nearly at my side as well, he spoke. "You'll be escorted to my lord's dwelling. Three of us will ride ahead of you and three behind. You may keep your swords, but they are to remain sheathed at all times." He seemed unsure of what to say next.

"What of basic introductions?" I said. "You seem like a civilized person in most other respects."

He stuttered a moment before receiving a nod from the soldier who was now on his right. "That is Torno," he said, pointing to the far left, "then Prodono, Tyren, Behrlak, Hahrno, and I am called Carlin."

"Carlin?" I said, surprised. "The same Carlin of whom our little friend spoke so admirably?"

"Did he speak of me that way?" Carlin said, looking downward as if ashamed. "I haven't had opportunity to talk to him since seeing him again early this morning, after such a long time apart."

"Then let's go and join him," Velarso said, having overheard this last exchange. "I'm Velarso. That's Ahdrynne, Nartok, and of course you've already met Ehrgsos."

"Very well then," I concluded. "I think we're all ready to join our little friend as well as the wizard-king about whom we've heard so much."

The trip up the mountain valley was rather long but we arrived at a most remarkable mountain fortress in time for a late midday meal.

Our little friend, would be along shortly, they assured me. There was much the king wanted to discuss with each and every one of us--most especially with the little Taevian.

CHAPTER 19

My Continuing Memories: Music in the Night

I'd awakened while it was still dark. The fire had gone out. The darkness faded slightly as my eyes adjusted to the dim light of the nearly full moon, still high in the night sky above me. Open spaces between the scattered trees were lit more brightly. My companions, Ahrynne, Ehrgsos, Velarso, and Nartok lay in shadow, sleeping soundly in a circle around me.

I heard a sound. My eyes shot open. I stared into the half-lit landscape around me. I recognized the strange melody of the old man in the cave, a faint, haunting music.

As silently as I could, I rose, carefully stepped over Ahdrynne's ankles, and moved away slowly. The music seemed to come from everywhere at first, then beckoned from the mountains to the southeast of our camp. The rising and falling tones were almost hypnotic, vibrating somberly into my ears and mind. I shook my head vigorously from side to side, but the sound persisted. With a deep breath, I gathered what determination I could and started off. I'd lived with too many questions for too long. I wanted some answers and expected to find them at the source of the strange music.

Gradually the music became more loud and clear. The farther I got from the camp, the more I hurried. The night was exceptionally quiet except for the soft whooshing of the wind stirring the trees and the crunching of pine needles and twigs beneath my feet. I slowed again to catch my breath. The ground grew more steep as I was led toward a narrow valley between two of the larger mountains. Before long, I was much further south than the narrow valley with the brook that Velarso, Ahdrynne, and I had followed earlier. I began to hurry again, afraid that the music would stop before I discovered its source, leaving me alone and probably unable to find my way back to our camp until morning.

A tiny trickle of water sparkled in the moonlight, flowing from a narrow gap between two house-sized boulders. The ground was fairly steep here as well. The music continued to weave its way through the unusually warm night from somewhere on the other side of the gateway between the boulders. The span between the two giant rocks was hardly more than twice as wide as I could reach. I glanced up before stepping through, and noticed the faintest glow of dawn edging its way into the sky.

Then I froze in my tracks and stared at a remarkably well-worn path of sand and small stones that led from the boulder on my left, upward and further back into the narrow space between the mountains. The path looked too well maintained to be any sort of natural animal trail or drainage. To the right of me, not too far off, I noticed a strange sort of shelf, both made of and supported by large tree trunks that had been stripped of all branches and cut to appropriate lengths. The shelf was covered with medium and small rocks. I drew nearer and noticed a couple of thick ropes looped around the supporting tree trunks, and realized the purpose of the construction. I stayed well away then, creeping along the left side of the inclined passage.

I glanced down when clear of the artificial avalanche and saw that a good jerk on the ropes and this steep valley could indeed be closed off to all but the most persistent attackers. I looked upward, but the mountainside was dark; I couldn't see anything. I continued onward and upward, noticing that the music had stopped.

The sky was growing bright now, the indigo hue of night giving way to the glowing flower of day. It finally occurred to me that my friends would awaken and be worried by my absence, but there was nothing I could do about that now. I probably should've wakened Velarso and asked him to come with me, but I was afraid he'd think it foolish to follow mysterious music through a nighttime landscape. He'd already put up with an unscheduled hike all the way to a summit, only because I'd insisted upon making the climb and in spite of the fact that I didn't have a good reason.

124

I still couldn't see any sign of a man-made structure, apart from the ropes that lay in plain sight on the other side of the water trickling quickly downward. The path I'd been following didn't seem to be approaching its end either. Only a few low bushes grew around me at this point. At last I was glad to be so short, being easily hidden by the dark foliage from any watchman peering down from above.

I glanced back a moment, then stopped to take a longer look. The flat plain visible between the precipitous peaks seemed to stretch into infinity and was rapidly turning to vibrant yellows, greens, and browns as the sun rose into view above and in front of me. I climbed higher.

There was something odd about a rock formation just ahead, but I wasn't sure just what. It looked like, no, it actually was. A great curving wall many times higher than a house had been built to span the steep depression between the mountains. In the middle about three-fourths of the way to the top of the man-made wall was a small pipe through which a trickle of water flowed to feed the tiny brook. At the end of the path, there was an arched doorway, just big enough for a man on horseback to pass through. I crouched behind a boulder next to the trail, then crept to the archway, hid in its shadow, and peered beyond.

A large lake with water clear as crystal lay just on the other side of the wall. Beyond the lake, the face of a building stood out of the rock like a gigantic relief sculpture. There were a few windows higher up, a couple of doors widely spaced from each other, and a few architectural refinements around some of the openings. The whole wonder blended into the natural contours of the mountain.

Then I saw some other dark shape, some combination of wood and glass, I think, but not like the two doors. This was on the opposite side of the lake from where I stood, in a place where the mountain curved toward me again so that the shape faced almost completely to the east. I scurried around the lake as quickly as possible, the area being so open that there was no way not to be seen by anyone who might be watching, since the sun had filled the space with light. Still there was no sound or movement. I approached with feelings of hope and of awe.

Fully in the beam of the morning sun stood a door five times my height and equally as wide. The painted windowpanes were bound in grey lead as smooth as a lady's hand-mirror. Such artistry seemed strange, or at least a jarring contrast to the rough, grey walls of the surrounding fortress.

I took hold of the door. It was hard to get a footing in the sandy soil. The oaken door began to budge and with a tired creak of its ancient hinges, I stumbled past into a dimly lit passageway. My long, gnarled fingers steadied me against damp, coarsely hewn walls while I strained my eyes at faint shadows just ahead. My oversized feet carried me deeper into the recesses of the fortress, tripping over cracks and crevices in the jagged limestone floor. Cool odors drifted into my nostrils and my ears wearied themselves to hear some small whisper of life. It was like walking through the previously undisturbed tomb of some ancient, forgotten ruler.

There! Faint strains of a lyre and someone singing. The labyrinth twisted to the left. Then I was falling, tumbling down, landing hard. I looked up at faces barely visible in the dim candle light. I'd found the great wizard-king at last.

From somewhere in the darkness came the question, "Who are you?" It echoed in my ears, as I groped within myself for a response.

CHAPTER 20

King Treston's Chapter

I stepped forward and extended a hand to the little creature on the floor, as he struggled to his feet again, before repeating the question I'd wanted to ask so many years before. "Who are you?"

"Judging by the golden staff upon which you lean, am I at last in the presence of King Treston?" a small voice replied.

"You are," I answered, "but not for the first time."

"Come, my lord, be seated." Trelm, a young page, appeared at my right, tugging my elbow gently toward the throne several paces behind me.

"We've met before?" the little one responded.

"Yes," I said, "but at the time we didn't speak the same language." The little creature's face registered great astonishment. "I meant you no harm, but was unwilling to be as honest with you as I should've been and," I paused, considering my next words and shaking my head. "Carlin misunderstood."

His eyes widened. "Carlin?"

"He's now one of my guards. He'd seen only thirteen summers when you first came to my castle, or rather, what used to be my castle," I said. A lingering memory of Castle Mirus distracted me momentarily. "The man who brought you to see me that first time has long since passed from this world to the next. Erundo, the duke of Rophalia, he was called. I understand we were correct in guessing that your ancestry is Taevian."

The little one nodded. "I first escaped from there only a short time before we first met." He'd inched his way across the room and stood only a couple of steps away. "After leaving you, I had many adventures and met many people, from whom I learned many things. Eventually, I met an archer, Gairen, who claimed to have served you until the Taevians overran your castle, forcing you to flee."

127

My eyes grew wide, hearing this. "How is Gairen? Is he safe?"

"First, a small bit of other news," the little one said. "A woman who rides the wind visited my friends and me, as we travelled to find you. She told us things that we could neither know nor learn by ourselves. By her report, Gairen escaped from a fierce battle by fleeing into the waters of the Bay of Brendwolt, and was carried to safety by means of a sea creature she sent to him."

"The woman's name," I asked, trying not to be impatient.

"Masra."

"Then she still lives." I had difficulty stifling an unceremonious laugh of pure joy.

"She said she's having trouble finding you." The little person added quickly. "She needs to be with you soon. Every day she's separated from you seems to add another year to her age." He paused. "Forgive me, your majesty, if I've spoken too boldly."

Slowly I stood to my feet again, knowing both the risks and the decision I was about to embrace. "I shall go out where she may find me," I announced.

The others in the room understandably reacted with great fear and concern.

Trelm rushed to the little one's side, imploring restraint. "My lord, you mustn't. To expose yourself would be to invite a Taevian attack. King Wolten is still alive and would be able to locate you at least as easily as Masra could."

"Forgive me, your majesty," the little one interrupted, "but how are these things possible?"

I smiled. "No, I don't suppose you've ever had opportunity to study such metaphysical marvels." I stepped forward, moving away from advisors, pages, and guards but motioning to the smallest person in the room to follow me. "The history is quite lengthy, but suffice to say that certain substances found in rocks and trees have the ability to either aid or hinder spiritual perception and ability--not completely, but significantly. The location of this fortress was chosen and its construction executed in such a way that we're visually and intuitively camouflaged and

128

thus almost completely undetectable to persons outside. What Trelm, my young page, fears, is that by making myself spiritually or psychically visible to Masra, that I'll also be detected by the king of Taevius."

"Would you be able to withstand him if he did attack with all the forces he could muster?"

I shrugged. "Uncertain."

"But my friends and the duke of Marhaéven were sure that..."

"You've met the duke of Marhaéven, have you?" I interjected and sighed. "One whom I found to be neither evil nor trustworthy." Another memory distracted me. "But who are these friends to whom you refer?"

"Four of them are yet at the feet of these mountains, probably very worried about me. They were all asleep when I slipped away from our camp last night and began my journey to here," he said as we came out into the light and strolled slowly around the lake. "I must return to them to let them know that I'm well."

"Better yet," I said, "I'll send some guards on horseback to fetch them. You and I must talk further, if I'm to be prepared for the consequences of revealing myself."

I turned and waved to Trelm, walking slowly about a half dozen paces behind us. He always brought a smile to my face, the way he went to extremes to watch over me like a mother hen while being young enough to almost be one of grandchildren. The youth scurried off at once and six mounted guards quickly appeared through one of the large wooden doors and trotted out of the fortress toward the valley below.

"What have I to offer, that you wish to speak with me further?" the little one said, when the guards had gone.

"I'm aware of a great disturbance in Taevius, and have been able to learn much concerning what transpired, the extent of damage done, and the emotional and spiritual climate that's fermenting there," I replied. His eyes met mine again. "I need a more precise rendering of the place, its people, and its most recent history. Anything at all that you can tell me would be helpful."

"Those whom I've met, who've also become good and loyal friends, have always referred to you as being a sort of wizard, someone with unexplainable powers and abilities. I'm skeptical that anything I could tell you would be of use. It's specifically because of your reputation as a wizard that I've sought you, in hopes that you may alter my appearance to something more pleasant," my small companion responded.

"You consider your appearance to be unpleasant?" I said, quite taken by surprise by the remark..

"You don't?" he responded with a puzzled expression on his wrinkled face.

I was silent for a long moment, choosing my words carefully. "We're alike, in that we both have much to learn and new things to discover about ourselves and our world." We sat down on a stone bench near the water's edge. "Who would you be if your stature, limbs, and features were not as they are?"

"Who would I be?" The little one seemed confused.

"Yes," I said lightly, "Who would you be?"

"Obviously, I've never known anything different."

"Would it be better, do you think, to be someone else?" I continued.

Still the little one seemed puzzled.

"For instance," I said, "tell me about the lives of your friends, at least as much as you know." He turned slightly sideways on the bench, facing me more directly.

His response was more directed to his answer than to my question. "I've yet to meet anyone who has enjoyed a truly trouble-free life. It can't be bought with money, it can't be built by human hands, and it can neither be demanded from nor given to friends or family."

"Yet you wish for me to change you into someone whom you're not," I said flatly.

"Is it so much to ask that the parts of my body be proportionate?" Irritation began creeping into his voice.

"Do you actually think that being differently proportioned has not shaped and molded everything about who you are and how you interact with everything around you?" I finally asked.

He was silent. "What would you do if I were to change your entire appearance this very moment?" I stood, took two quick steps away, whirled to face him again, and raised my arms high, as if about to cast a spell of some sort. Instinctively perhaps, he jumped back and dropped out of sight behind a nearby boulder. I smiled and lowered my arms. "You see? Some things make better fantasies than realities." He peeked out from behind the boulder as I stroked my chin thoughtfully. "It was many years ago that my father taught me that all things exist for a reason and exist as they are for a reason too. I would do you no kindness if I were to magically change you."

The little one's shoulders sank at these words.

"I heard your poem yesterday on the mountaintop," I said, trying to put a more positive spin on the situation. "The depth of understanding required to group such ideas and compose such phrases seems inconsistent with a request to be physically altered for no other reason than the acceptance and approval of others."

"Yet I have never understood why a person such as I would be born in Taevius," he mumbled.

"In the wrong place and time, a blessing is a burden. In the right place and time, a blessing is essential," I explained. "I believe it to be a pure fact that you are a blessing."

I stared at him for a moment longer. He looked away, then back to me again, seeming to soften a little, hopefully feeling a little less oppressed by his body, considering my words. I hoped I'd said the right thing.

"You call me a blessing," he said at last.

I nodded, then smiled. He stepped to the water's edge to stare at his reflection. It seemed wise to leave him alone with his thoughts and emotions, so I slipped away silently.

I closed the door with stained glass panes and went up a side passage to watch from a small window. The little one continued to stare at his reflection in the surface of the lake, then ran his fingers over the contours of his face and ears. Then he slowly extended a hand toward the reflection. The water rippled as his fingers connected with its surface and he jumped back, as if waking from dream. He looked around quickly and I wondered if my moment of spying wasn't somehow a little bit rude.

131

"Is everything all right, my lord?" Trelm appeared at the end of the side passageway.

"Uh, yes, of course," I stuttered, momentarily embarrassed. "Would you go out to our little friend by the lake, please, and bring him to the dining room so that he and I might talk a little bit more before the midday meal?"

"Of course, my lord."

I watched another moment or two as Trelm approached the little one, who was again staring at his reflection. The page touched the little one's shoulder gently but had apparently not been heard approaching, judging by a second startled reaction. I hurried back to the room where we'd met earlier.

I made a point of smiling when Trelm and the little one entered the room and gestured to the chair on the opposite side of the table. "I trust this has been a fruitful day for you, little traveller."

"Yes," he whispered, nodding.

"Having thought the whole matter over one more time, I have concluded that you're probably right, that there's nothing more to know about the Taevian forces or strategies that would help." I said. "We both know only too well the strength and manner of what we're up against." The little one seemed confused. "I'm afraid your friends exaggerated my abilities," I explained.

"Your majesty," he said, "I'm no general, I've never even been a soldier, but I learned from Sir Trendall, my friend the knight, that a mixture of wisdom and perseverance gains the true victory. Appearances can be disappointing at first glance--I should know--but you've got to try to take whatever you've got to offer and see how it comes out. Nothing is categorically impossible."

"I guess it's my turn to be discouraged. Perhaps if Masra were here..." I said, slipping into another wistful distraction.

"Then get her here," he said firmly. "You told me you know how. Maybe her ability to ride the wind would come in handy."

"Well that much I can do myself, but I don't want to spend the rest of my life running away," I replied.

"You can ride the wind too?" he interrupted.

132

"It's not that difficult. Anyone could do it," I said, shrugging slightly.

"So teach everyone here to do it. Taevians only use handheld weapons. We could fly over their heads out of reach." He smiled a little and I couldn't help but smile as well, at his somewhat naive enthusiasm..

"Masra could help me, but what she and I know how to do isn't actually flying in the way that you seem to think. In any case," I said, as I began to remember, "we do have some surprises that should even the odds a bit."

CHAPTER 21

My Continuing Memories: Friendships

My friends had arrived while the king and I were talking. We went to join them in the great hall where a midday meal was being served. Velarso snatched me immediately into one of his great bear-hugs, finally releasing me to reprimand me for going off alone without leaving any word concerning my whereabouts and safety. I explained all that had transpired during my absence. King Treston watched and smiled as he ate, perhaps amused and pleased by the strong bonds of friendship I evidently shared with the four guards.

When I'd finished speaking, the king began his address to all present. "I trust then, that you all understand that in order for me to contact Masra, I must accept the threat of Taevian attack. I hope that you'll all be willing to help in whatever ways you can."

"Rest assured that we will do no dishonorable thing while we're your guests," Ehrgsos replied, "but it was my understanding that Taevius was destroyed in the avalanche."

"The avalanche was a great blow to the strength of the Taevian forces," the king replied, "but in actuality, only about two-thirds of the city was destroyed and about half its population survived. That they wish to take revenge on Nypothnia goes without saying."

For a moment, the room was filled with silence. Nartok was the first to speak again. "Just exactly how many Taevian soldiers are we expecting to engage in combat?"

King Treston clearly didn't want to answer but finally conceded, "Approximately five thousand."

A loud, collective gasp rose from nearly everyone in the room.

"That's a hundred to one," Hahrno commented quietly.

Ahdrynne grinned. "So what's the secret weapon that allows you to even consider such a conflict?"

135

The king seemed somehow relieved. "Actually, we have a fair number of unconventional weapons at our disposal. The odds may very well be evenly matched."

"So when do we begin to learn about these new weapons," asked Velarso.

"Tomorrow morning. Tonight, I must open the door to contact with Masra." The king gathered his thoughts a moment. "She will be a great asset, since she's already familiar with all the things I'll be describing to you."

"Not to mention," Torno said with a sheepish grin, "that you love her and long to be with her again."

King Treston smiled, blushing ever so slightly.

"Why not contact her now?" I suggested.

"The light of the moon is needed," the king replied. "We must wait until the day's light is gone from the sky. If you'll excuse me, I'll go and make preparations, using the resources of alchemy and literature available to me." He quietly left the room. I noticed he was no longer walking with the aid of his golden staff, and seemed to have new energy in his steps.

The guards began chattering among themselves like a bunch of old school chums, finally leaving the room for a tour of the fortress, conducted by Hahrno. Only Carlin stayed behind. Something was evidently troubling him, judging by the way he had stared at me from time to time during the meal. I smiled, trying to read his eyes for some clue.

"I thought about you frequently after you left," he said at last, "wondering whether you were well and safe or how someone of your size and limitations could survive what I knew to be a mostly unfriendly land."

We stared into each other's eyes for a long moment. "I met a great many oppressive people," I answered, "but also a few like yourself, with good hearts and virtuous spirits." He made no reply so I continued. "I've never told you of the world to which I was born, the world which I fled. Suffice to say that it was a good deal more harsh and unfriendly than anything I've encountered in my travels."

136

He seemed a bit relieved. "I learned later that you would've been safe with us if I hadn't encouraged you to leave. I'm sorry to have put you through whatever evils you encountered."

"No matter, my friend," I said. He looked up suddenly and smiled when he heard the word "friend." "It's the very evils of which you speak that have helped me to become the one who stands before you." I wet my lips and gathered my thoughts. "I might have only the understanding and strength of a child if I hadn't gone forward, through each hardship and challenge."

"Yet there's something about you," he said, puzzled, "that yet reflects the honesty and purity of a child."

"You flatter me," I said, laughing. "I'm no saint."

"I envy the way you approach things with simple and honest confidence. It seems that every decision or action I make is burdened with context and implication." He shook his head. "You're so free. I'm beset with responsibilities and relationships that greatly limit my freedom of choice."

"But it's those responsibilities and relationships that give direction and purpose to life," I said. He seemed unconvinced. "I've spent my life searching for an understanding of what life is, of who I am, and of what the two have to do with each other. If you envy the life that I've led, know that I envy the life that you've lived. Still, I wouldn't want to trade places with you. By the help of your lord, of the many friends I've found, and even by your help as well, I'm finally learning to appreciate just being me."

"I'm restless," Carlin replied.

"And well you should be," I said. "A young man with his life before him and his destiny yet to claim." I went to stand next to him. "All things in good time, my friend."

He smiled as I gave him a forgiving hug.

Loud chuckling in one of the passageways told us the other guards were returning.

"So here you are," Velarso said, beaming. "This is quite a place. There's even a winding stair to the very top of the mountain."

"And a huge stable," Nartok added excitedly.

"And a strange kind of garden from which everyone here is fed," Ahdrynne chimed in.

"There are actually about fifty men living here," said Prodono.

"Our wise master has made us more self-sufficient than I ever thought possible," said Behrlak. "Before coming to live with him here, that is."

"It makes me both happy and sad," I said, not meaning to bring an end to their frivolous mood. New and old friends stared with expressions of bafflement. "The duke of Marhaéven told of a former time when knowledge was much more than it generally is," I explained. "He said that King Treston has presumably the largest remnant of that knowledge. I mourn the loss of what must've been a great amount of wisdom and understanding, a precious victim of the dark time in which we live. We've forgotten so very much."

"I look forward to the time when all is recovered," said Ehrgsos. "I trust that it will be."

Small, determined smiles crept onto their faces, then we followed Carlin's suggestion of a walk around the lake in the late afternoon sun.

King Treston was there, studying something about the construction of the wall intently, finally nodding. Tyren went to him to learn what he was about or whether he needed assistance with any task.

"Yes," he said at last, when the rest of us stood closer to him also. "The horses must be moved to the upper stable and the pathway door to the valley sealed up, but first make sure that the ropes to the lower gate are in good working order."

It seemed a strange way to proceed, but no one questioned the wisdom of the king. Hahrno and Prodono headed off to tend to the horses, with Torno and Tyren trailing behind to secure two horses with which to go and check the condition of the ropes. The upper ends of the ropes were securely fastened to a large cairn, higher on the mountainside above the door with stained-glass panes, thus reaching over the top of the wall. Behrlak and Carlin were instructed to gather some of the other men who were tending to the garden or other areas of the fortress to assist them in emptying the lower rooms of the fortress of all belongings and provisions of any kind.

"What of us," Velarso said. "Is there nothing we can do?"

"Do you have a good swimmer among you?" King Treston asked.

Ahdrynne was already undressing as he asked what the specific task was to be.

"You may have noticed a pipe in the wall as you entered this fortress, through which the trickle of water which runs to the valley flows," the king replied. "It must be sealed from this side. I have a small metal cap in my room that will fit tightly but I think with not too much difficulty over the pipe's end, which is located in the center of the wall at about the same level as the surface of the lake."

"No problem," Ahdrynne replied.

The cap was brought to him and he dove in without hesitation. His head appeared suddenly above the water's surface a second later. "Ah! This water is very, very cold."

We laughed at the unexpected amusement, but King Treston remained quite serious. "Will you be all right?"

"No problem," he said and began stroking strongly toward the location King Treston had described. My friends and I grew quiet, then began fidgeting.

"What do we do if he gets too cold or tired? Is there any rope or boat or anything by which to rescue him?" Velarso asked very quietly.

"He's reached the wall." I almost shouted. Ahdrynne seemed to be struggling, first moving a little to one side, then toward the other. Suddenly he took two strong strokes toward his left, having apparently found the overflow pipe. Then he began swimming back towards us.

"Mission accomplished," he called between gasps for air, when he was only a short distance from us. Nartok took a couple steps out into the lake and grabbed Ahdrynne's hand the moment he was within reach. Drinlar took a step into the water to help them both ashore. Trelm was waiting with a thick blanket as the three stepped out of the water.

"It's sealed all right," Ahdrynne gasped, once he was wrapped though still shivering within the blanket.

"Good," King Treston said, watching the sun's last orange beams fading from the valley in the distance. "As soon as Torno and Tyren return from checking the ropes, wall up the entrance to this fortress, being certain to completely fill the space with the heaviest boulders, sand, and mud you can manage. In only a few more hours I'll be able to call Masra. Then we must prepare ourselves for a battle that could alter the course of history for all of Nypothnia."

CHAPTER 22

Hahrno's Chapter

The sun was gone and tiny stars began to glow within the twilight above us. A cool breeze stirred the air. King Treston sat on a large boulder at the mountaintop's highest point, staring into the darkness pensively. A couple dozen paces distant, encircling him on almost three sides, every man living in the fortress watched in silence, sometimes looking off to the west toward Taevius. The night felt warm and comforting, but filled with energy.

"Harhrno?" Nartok whispered from just behind me. "Are weird things like this common here?"

"I'm not sure what you mean," I answered.

"Everyone gathering to stare up at the stars and wait for who knows what to happen. Maybe I'm the only one, but this is really different from anything I've ever been a part of."

"Hmm. There was a time," I replied to Nartok, "when it would've been me asking your question. The last several years serving the king, however, has brought much stranger things than this into my life. Perhaps it isn't typical or common," I conceded, "but it's nothing for you to worry about just the same. In time everything will make more sense to you."

"Your majesty," the little one said, climbing onto a rock at the king's elbow, "I've been pondering this former time of civilization of which I've been told. Sometimes I have dreams of things I've never seen or heard, and I wonder if somehow I'm remembering things that I know haven't existed since long before I was born." He paused, perhaps waiting for a reply. "I wonder how what I've just said could be true, yet somehow I know that it is." King Treston smiled briefly and glanced toward the small misshapen person. "I was told that the civilized world fell because it was overwhelmed by the sheer number of the enemy."

The king shook his head slowly, again smiling slightly. "That," he said, "would be much too easy an explanation. The civilized world, as it is and was called, was very weak by reason of certain dependencies. Marvelous machines and inventions were prevalent and created many abilities and opportunities that have been lost, but the greatest loss was within the people themselves. They'd impoverished themselves in the proliferation of what they called, 'technology.' Even before this technology was lost, all that wasn't concrete had already been lost."

"Not concrete?" the little one said.

"A person may know a great many facts and possess a great many abilities, but have no perception of spiritual and emotional realities which, in actuality, are far more enduring." King Treston took a moment to scan the fading glow along the western horizon. "We see and hear and feel only the most tiny part of all that exists. Too often we live with only what's easy and comfortable. The people of Avinngra had forgotten all those things that give meaning and purpose to life. Their lives had motion, but not life."

"Life without life," the little one said. "Perhaps existence without awareness?"

The king nodded slowly. "They had no understanding or knowledge or ability to support themselves without the presence of all their precious toys. The conquest of Avinngra was easy once the invaders had severed lines of communication and energy. It was, as they say, 'a great tragedy waiting to happen.'"

"Lines of energy?" the little one asked.

King Treston sighed. "Suffice to say that the people of that time possessed wonders that are now too difficult to explain, even if we could legitimately claim to understand."

The only sound in the silence that followed was the faint hum of the wind over rocky cliffs and crevices around us.

"I was horrified the first time I saw my reflection," the little misshapen creature said. "I think I believed myself to be evil or bad in some way, to look as I do."

"And yet," King Treston replied, "you exist. As does Taevius, as did Avinngra, as will people and civilizations and mountains and valleys and animals and trees and all sorts of other things in years to come."

The little one tipped his head to the side again, perhaps confused.

"All things exist in their place and time," the king explained, "and are essential and good in some way."

"But why?" the little one responded.

"It isn't always so important to know the reason, as to know that there is a reason," King Treston answered.

The little one looked down before continuing to speak. "I suppose there are a great many things beyond the reach of our current understanding and perception."

"It's time," King Treston announced and stood to his feet.

The wind grew much stronger, swirling the king's long robes around him in the growing moonlight. The little one scrambled back to where Nartok and I stood, listening and watching. Velarso and Ehrgsos came quickly to stand next to us also.

"What's happening?" Velarso asked.

"I don't know," the little one stammered nervously, "he just said 'it's time' and stood up."

"Everything's okay," I reassured them. "Just relax and watch what happens."

The wind was growing very strong now, urging everyone except King Treston to huddle deeper into crevices and behind rocks for protection, but with our eyes fixed on the wizard-king bathed in moonlight.

He raised his arms wide, like great wings. he seemed to glow with more than just moonlight. He took a small crystal of some sort from somewhere inside of his robe and raised it over his head, where it caught the moon's bright rays and magnified them to the brilliance of a star in the wizard's hand. Slowly he turned a full circle, then pulled his hand downward, leaving the glowing crystal to float in the air over his head, unaffected by the thundering winds that enveloped the mountaintop. The star-crystal began to rise higher and higher, seeming to grow brighter and brighter. In moments, I couldn't distinguish it from the other stars, which filled the sky in a greater profusion than I'd ever seen.

Then she was there, stepping into the moonlight as if from some deep shadow. Even having seen numerous wonders

143

performed by King Treston already, I gasped at the glow on their faces, a glow which revealed remarkably youthful features. A meeting of smiles and sparkling eyes, the first caressing touch of strong, young hands, then a kiss, and the celebration of an embrace. I shook my head to regain my senses and noticed all the others staring open-mouthed at the reunion as well.

Perhaps time stopped. I don't know how long we all sat there, transfixed in the moonlight. Perhaps we would've been there longer, but a dark cloud crept over the moon and the lovers, startled, parted to face the cloud. They held hands, facing away from us, and appeared to be listening to something I couldn't hear. Then they nodded silently toward the cloud and turned back toward the rest of us, nodding and smiling briefly toward the little one in particular before climbing down off of the large boulder. The king escorted his queen to the top of the stairs that led back into the fortress, with the rest of us following close behind.

We gathered in a spacious hall not far below the top of the mountain where numerous candles were already burning. Two ornately carved chairs at the far end of the room were occupied by the now-youthful royal couple, while the rest of us chose various places along the walls or on the floor.

"It's so good to have you back," Treston said to Masra, then turned to the rest of us. "As you've been told, I have probably made our presence and location known to the enemy in order to effect the miracle you've all witnessed this night. If we don't find ourselves under attack within a week, I'll be very much surprised." He paused a moment, evidently to let the last statement sink into our bewildered minds. "If anyone wishes to leave this place in the hope of preserving his life, he's free to do so with a week's provisions at his side. But he would have to climb out by whatever route he can find. I can't offer a horse since the wall to the valley has been sealed and no route of escape suitable for a horse remains, until such time as the way is cleared again. The overflow pipe from the lake has been sealed and the lower chambers are slowly being flooded even as we speak."

"Are we in danger here?" Prodono said tentatively.

"No," the king responded, "the water won't rise high enough to threaten either us or the horses, which are now in the upper stable, or the garden either, for that matter. But to return to my first concern. If any wish to leave, it shall be that man's choice and none is allowed to show any disapproval to the man who makes such a choice."

A long silence met the king's gentle gaze around the room. "To reassure those who've decided to stay," he continued, "Masra and I will seek to impart to you any and all abilities that may help you in the coming conflict. If anyone has any idea or suggestion for our defense..."

"Or conquest," interrupted Carlin, bringing a resolute silence to the room again for a brief moment.

King Treston forced a smile. "Or conquest of the enemy who's sure to come, please don't hesitate to speak with me." A heavy silence hung over the room. Finally he took a deep breath and closed by saying, "Then let's all retire to bed, get plenty of rest, and be prepared for a day of rigorous training and preparation when the sun rises again."

The king and queen remained seated, looking about somewhat tensely as the men filed out. Noticing the little one lingering behind, I waited so that I could show him to a sleeping chamber. "Your majesties," he called quietly from the dark corner where he stood, "I'm puzzled by my role in the forthcoming conflict, yet I know somehow that I'm needed here."

They looked at each other for a moment, as if reading each other's thoughts.

Masra turned to answer first. "When the time comes, you'll do what must be done. No one will need to tell you what to do or be. No answer is needed until the question finally presents itself."

"Trust yourself to do what's right and good," King Treston added. "Everything shall be as it should be, as in some secret way it already is." The little one nodded understanding after a moment and the king and queen smiled in return, stood, and left the room.

The little one and I remained alone with the still-burning candles. He stepped back against a wall and slid to the floor,

145

staring at a particular candle flame, perhaps unaware that I'd stayed behind as well. I noticed his eyelids drooping, went to him and touched his shoulder lightly.

He jerked awake again. I smiled to reassure him. "Come to bed, little friend. I'm sure we can find something more comfortable than this stone corner."

He seemed only half-awake so I chuckled softly as I lifted me from the floor and carried him to a bed, quietly blowing out most of the candles as we passed them. He was already asleep when I lay down beside him and Velarso. I looked at the strange wrinkled little face one more time before closing my eyes and saw a peculiar twitch, accompanied by a quiet whimper. I wondered what a person such as he would dream about. I laid my hand on his shoulder once, offering brief comfort to him even as he slept, then rolled over to get some rest myself.

CHAPTER 23

My Continuing Memories: Preparations

As if standing in the middle of a cloud, everywhere I looked I saw only a thick, white mist, slowly swirling around me. The ground beneath my feet was brown and dry, like the central meeting place in Taevius, or the floor of my father's house where I'd been chained not so long ago.

I heard the dull scuffling of footsteps in the dust and whirled to see the wizard-king, Treston, appear behind me, young and strong but strangely silent, with an intense light in his eyes. We stared. Then I heard another scuffling noise and turned to see the king of Taevius, Wolten, step into view, the same resolute, confrontational light in his eyes. I looked from one to the other, waiting for an explanation of some kind, but the only sound was the distant hushing of the wind.

Again, I heard the scuffling of feet. This time it was my mother, with a faint smile on her face. She actually even looked pretty. I'd never seen my mother smile, or look pretty, or show any indication of genuine life. Her easy smile turned to a tight-lipped one then, and she gestured for me to turn around once more. There stood my father.

Standing a dozen paces away, like the four points of the compass, these four elders stared at me as I glanced from one to another, anxious to know what all of this could mean. The soft, glowing mist still swirled around us, ever so slowly and gently, leaving clear only the circle we occupied.

My father spoke to me at last. "I didn't understand, but then, neither did you."

I responded with a gesture indicating confusion.

"You're my son and I mistook the honor for a curse."

"It's an honor to have a son who's deformed?" I said.

"It's an honor to have a son who's like none other," my father responded, "a son who will dare what so few will."

I shrugged. "What have I ever dared that's even noteworthy?"

My father smiled briefly and shook his head. "You're such a boy yet," he said, out loud but to himself. "You've travelled far and engaged the friendship of people I've never imagined. Safe within that which was familiar and comfortable to me, I avoided the experience of life itself."

"And yet you are alive?" I said.

"When the avalanche began, we feared we'd angered our gods and were being punished. In the midst of the thunder of falling rock, I was stricken with fear that you'd be killed. Our house stood so close to the chasm's wall that it was buried when I reached the spot after the dust had settled. I'm sure the others thought me mad, as I dug and clawed a passage to the door of the house. I suppose I should've been angry when I understood that you were linked to the cause of the avalanche, but I remember feeling only relief that your broken body wasn't there."

I'd never heard my father speak this way. His eyes seemed wet, but I simply couldn't believe there might be tears in my father's eyes. Avoiding the unfamiliar depth of emotion between us, I simply asked, "And then?"

My father looked away for a moment, stuttered, and began again. "The others were gathering to retaliate. I just stared at the emptiness of my house from where I sat by the hearth, thinking. When I finally came out, everyone was gone--well, almost everyone." His eyes shot across to my mother's face. "I heard a mournful voice in the distance, singing something. It was your mother. She looked at me in a new way that day. "

We both glanced to my mother, who smiled bashfully in response.

"I guess I looked at her in a new way that day too," he said. "Then we left Taevius."

"You left Taevius?" I said in astonishment.

"Yes." My father paused, eyeing me skeptically. "You did. Why not us?

My tongue moved in my mouth, but I had no answer.

"We journeyed to the east," my mother said, "far, far to the east. Even farther than where you are."

"You know where I am?"

She smiled. "A mother knows many things in ways that no one can explain. You don't need to come to us. You need to lead your own life." Her voice had begun to echo strangely, as if coming from deep within a cave. She paused. "We're very proud of you."

My mouth hung open for a long moment.

"We're doing well," my father said. His voice had also taken on the strange echo. "The first few weeks among strange people, to whom we were equally as strange, I'm sure, were difficult. But we have many friends now and life is quite different than it was in Taevius."

"There's so much I've always wanted to say to you," I said, at last finding my voice again.

"It's unnecessary," my mother said. "Understanding passes between hearts without words being spoken, if we're only able to listen. Too often there are distractions." Her voice echoed so much that I was almost unable to understand her words.

"We're in your heart and mind forever," my father said. "And you are in ours. Our spirits will take joy from the happiness of yours. Go, be blessed in all you do, and know that our love is with you always." He said something else also, but the echo had increased and I couldn't make out his final words.

I started to speak but he smiled and stepped back, fading into the mist. I turned quickly, but my mother was already gone too.

I glanced to King Wolten and King Treston, but they remained stone-faced and silent.

"What's the meaning of all this?" I shouted. I shook my hands over my head and screamed again, "What's the meaning of all this?"

Tears started running down my cheeks. I moved toward the wizard-king and instantly he was gone. I turned just in time to see the king of Taevius vanish also. I swung around, frantically looking this way and that as the mist continued to swirl about me, slowly getting closer and closer, the clear inner circle where I stood growing smaller and smaller. I closed my eyes and screamed.

"Wake up, my friend!"

149

My eyes shot open to Velarso's worried face, barely visible in the dim candlelight. I was gasping for breath. We were in a small room with Hahrno and Ehrgsos, who stared at me with fear in their eyes.

"It was only a bad dream," Velarso said, hugging me to his strong, naked chest.

Ehrgsos came over to put his hand on my shoulder, then Hahrno also. I leaned back to wipe the tears from my face. Ehrgsos and Hahrno stepped back, looking from Velarso to me and back to Velarso, who nodded reassuringly for them to go back to bed. Ehrgsos stepped back and sat on the edge of his bed, but kept his eyes on us for another long moment. Hahrno lay down on his side, facing us, but didn't close his eyes.

My heart was beating fast. The dream had seemed so real, so incredibly vivid. Scenes and words began replaying themselves in my mind as Velarso continued to hold me, offering whatever comfort he could. I snuggled deeper into his arms, trying unsuccessfully to block the images from my mind.

I remember being awake in his arms for quite some time, but must have finally drifted off to sleep again. I opened my eyes to hear many footsteps in the hallway. Hahrno and Ehrgsos had already gone, evidently to breakfast. Velarso still slumbered quietly, his arms wrapped around me, a beautifully peaceful expression on his face. I put my head against his chest again, and the movement woke him. I looked up to see him smiling. I smiled too, to tell him that everything was okay again, although I still didn't understand the images I remembered from the dream.

At breakfast, the chatter around the table focused on what the day would bring. Everyone seemed excited and in good spirits. Ehrgsos gave me a sideways glance and a quick smile when Velarso and I entered the room, but nothing more was said about the previous night in our sleeping chamber.

Prodono came in when all had nearly finished eating, and said that we were to gather on the mountain's summit. A large area had been prepared there for the training we were to receive today. I noticed Ehrgsos talking to Ahdrynne and Nartok as the others began to file out of the room and up the stairs, gesturing toward me and apparently causing the worried expressions on my other two friends' faces. I looked down, somewhat embarrassed, and Nartok was suddenly by my side.

"You do know that we're your friends," he said. "You can talk to us about anything that's bothering you."

I smiled and fidgeted, unsure of what to say. "It was just a very strange dream. I'm sorry to have been a bother."

"No, no, it's quite all right," Aldern said, now standing at Nartok's shoulder. "Just let us know how we can help if anything ever comes up that you want to talk about."

I forced a smile and nodded to each of them thankfully. Then we joined the other men outside.

Carlin saw us emerge from the top of the stairs and smiled and waved. King Treston was about to begin his explanation of the day's activity. Queen Masra was seated only a couple paces from his side.

"I've described our situation to the queen in detail and we discussed possibilities until almost morning," the king began, "so please forgive us if we seem a bit weary. We're starting with the most difficult piece of our defense, and I'm not sure exactly how this will be used when the enemy arrives, but we want to give you as many resources as possible."

The queen smiled, stood up, and stepped to her husband's side. "What Treston refers to, is what may be called, 'riding the wind.' It's a largely forgotten means of moving quickly from one place to another, but it only works in places where wind may blow, and there's also no true consciousness or awareness of surroundings while in flight, so to speak." She gazed around at the men for a moment before continuing. "Carlin," she called, "if you'll please distribute the Aftresian amulets." Then she turned to speak to the men in general. "Aftresia is a rare crystal possessing the power to amplify mental energies. By thinking of **a specific place to be, focusing on it to the extreme of momentarily discarding awareness of your physical body, you'll find yourself in the new place of which you were thinking.** Usually it helps to close your eyes while making the jump from one place to another, such that it may seem like slowly blinking your eyes and finding yourself in another place."

"Of course, the hard part," King Treston said, "is to close your eyes in order to make such an escape when an enemy is bearing down on you with a raised sword. Those who are too dependent on eyesight have the most difficulty benefitting from the power of this crystal."

"I'm not sure what other explanation I can offer," Queen Masra concluded, "so once you have the amulet strung about your neck, you're free to begin practicing. You'll see a large number of rocks painted with symbols, scattered around the top of this mountain. These are practice targets for you to use."

"We'll wander among you, offering what advice or encouragement we can," the king concluded.

With that, a quiet murmuring rose from the men gathered around. Some were obviously skeptical, some willing to try, and some convinced that the king's every word was universal law.

"So what do you think?" I asked Carlin, when he got to me.

"I don't know," he responded, "I've seen a lot of incredible things, last night being not the least of the wonders King Treston has performed." He scratched his head a moment. "I suppose I'd have to concede that anything's possible, but it's probably more complicated than it sounded just now when Queen Masra explained it."

He moved along, handing out the amulets. I peered into the strange translucence of the crystal, a kind of murky mixture of blue and red about the size of a man's fingernail, then lifted the thin cord over my head.

Ahdrynne was the first to "fly." First he was here and then he was there. Mouths fell open in amazement.

"It's easy," he declared, "just don't let your brain get in the way."

"Skepticism is easier denounced than discarded," the queen chided. "Let no one who encounters difficulty be discouraged."

Within the hour, perhaps half of those gathered had managed at least one short "flight," aided by individual counseling from either the king or queen. Those who just couldn't seem to succeed in the effort were encouraged to focus on other means of defense. Carlin was among those having difficulty and was growing quite frustrated indeed, when King Treston interrupted the disordered group to announce that Tyren would now lead a session aimed at perfecting sword-handling skills.

Tyren began by speaking of balance, anticipation, and the advantages and disadvantages of basic defense and attack positions, demonstrating with the aid of Behrlak.

Then Hahrno gave brief tips on effectively defending against an enemy bearing a sword, when one is armed only with a staff or spear. After a light midday meal, Torno worked with the men individually, honing the accuracy of each one's archery skills. The entirety of the arsenal of the fortress was brought out, each weapon described and its use instructed as the day wore on. King Treston and Queen Masra reappeared just before dusk with more amulets in their hands.

"These," he said, "bear the Methryzite crystal, which can render its bearer invisible when standing perfectly still. There is also a small Tyrib stone attached, which discourages injury in battle."

"Again," she reminded, "they amplify your own thoughts and beliefs. What's true within your mind becomes more obvious to those around you. Each stone has both abilities and limitations, so use them wisely so that they serve as an advantage and not as a disadvantage."

"If the abilities of which we speak elude you," King Treston cautioned, "don't let your heart be discouraged. The abilities that each of you do possess are essential to the triumph that must take place."

The whole business of crystals giving special abilities to the bearer struck me as kind of bizarre and hard to take seriously, and for the briefest moment I wondered if it wasn't a cruel trick offering false hope. But then, I'd seen Ahdrynne fly, so there had to be at least something to it.

As the others began descending into the fortress, I stepped away to the western edge of the summit to gaze at the faint orange glow of the sun setting across the plain. King Treston came to stand by my side when the others had gone. A few moments of silence passed.

"I had a strange dream last night," I said. "In the dream, I spoke with my mother and father, but two others who were there refused to say anything--King Wolten and you." I turned to find him staring into the distance with the same kind of intense expression he'd had in my dream.

Finally, he turned his eyes to the ground. "You've heard the story of the rise and fall of what's called the civilized time in Nypothnia. What the duke of Marhaéven didn't tell you is that the first person put into Taevius was Traénon of Syldonia's brother."

"How could someone hate his brother so?" I responded in amazement.

"The seeds of hate." The king sighed and shook his head. "No one's ever really figured that one out. We can describe and speculate and explain endlessly, but a final answer always seems to elude us. Traénon never confided to even his closest advisors just what had come between him and his brother."

"What was the brother's name? Does anyone know?"

He smiled briefly, as if strangely amused. "Our world is much more interconnected than most realize. The brother's name was Brendwolt. Perhaps it was a faint glimmer of forgiveness that made Traénon name that bay after his brother, some tiny desire to honor his brother in some way." He paused, pursed his lips, and added, "Still, the Bay of Brendwolt is just about as far from the ruins of Avinngra as you can get."

"So," I said, "you're directly descended from Traénon and the King Wolten is directly descended from Brendwolt. The whole of the land and its people are violently divided by a long-forgotten rivalry between siblings."

King Treston nodded sadly, a look of longing in his eyes. "Perhaps one day I'll be given a chance for reconciliation with my distant cousin. If not me, perhaps my children and his."

"A day of confrontation may be sooner than you think," I said nervously in the gathering darkness. "Aren't those campfires on the horizon?"

"Yes," he said slowly, turning his eyes to the objects at which I pointed, "hundreds of them."

154

CHAPTER 24

Carlin's Chapter

"Hopefully everyone was able to get a good night's sleep, especially considering the announcement I need to make," King Treston said at breakfast the next morning. "The little one and I observed hundreds of campfires in the distance last night. I think there is little doubt that the Taevian army is rapidly approaching." The silence was tense.

"My lord?" I asked, breaking the stillness.

"Yes, Carlin?"

"The obvious question, how long until they're here?"

"Perhaps three to four hours," the king answered. "Maybe less, maybe more. Suffice to say that the hour of reckoning has come, perhaps sooner than we'd prefer." The King Treston's gaze scanned the candle-lit room for reactions. Receiving none, he continued. "Behrlak will need at least nine others to help him seal the path to this fortress with our artificially induced avalanche, as soon as the Taevians approach the narrow stone gate where our mountain meets the plain. Torno will oversee the placement of as many bows, arrows, and spears as we possess on the high ridges at each side of the wall that restrains the lake. Hahrno and Carlin will coordinate lines of supply for those on the forward line of defense, carrying additional weapons, food, water, and messages as needed.

The king paused a long moment, then glanced to the queen and concluded in a low, tense voice, almost a whisper. "Now go, and may all that's good be with each and every one of you."

Instantly, the room was filled with activity. In the briefest of moments, it was silent again. Only King Treston, Queen Masra, the little one and I remained.

"Have I sent these loyal friends to their deaths?" The king said, to no one in particular.

The queen's hand touched his shoulder and they looked at each other without saying a word.

155

"Perhaps," the little one responded, "and perhaps not. Destiny hasn't yet laid the final card upon the table. Anything is still possible."

"Remember, Treston," Masra said, "that each has made and must continue to make the choices with which he's content to live."

"Or by which he's content to die," King Treston replied somberly.

"Let's go to the top of the mountain," the little one suggested. "We'll be able to see how the battle progresses. Good or bad, the choices have been made; it remains only for each to do his best."

The couple looked to one another, then to the little one and I, finally nodding and rising from their seats to climb the stairs to the summit. There was nothing more to say.

"In a sense," the king said as we stepped into the bright open air, "we've put ourselves into a corner with no escape but riding the wind--of which not all have proven to be capable. We'll see whether the corner we've chosen is sufficiently defendable."

They went to stand on the brow of the peak, facing west, Masra resting her head on Treston's shoulder. Below were rows of archers and swordsmen, most also looking west, at a large cloud of dust rising into the otherwise clear air. The little one went to stand near them, gazing down at friends on the ridges below, waiting for the enemy to come within range of our defenses. I chose a high boulder a few paces to the right of the king, having been selected to stand closest to the couple and be their last defending champion should the Taevian forces get that far. Velarso turned and saw the four of us watching from above, waved to us, and smiled briefly. No one said a word, the gravity of the moment weighing us into silence.

A distant drumming sound carried over the wind. I noticed the little one looking at the three stones strung about his neck and glanced down at the stones hanging against my own chest, wishing and hoping for I don't know what. The opposing force seemed to move toward us with agonizing slowness. In our minds, we were already deep in combat.

The enemy seemed to grow continuously more numerous, more ominous. They seemed to stretch almost from the foot of the mountain to the western horizon. We numbered between fifty and sixty persons. What hope did we actually have? Yet I knew from past observation of King Treston that an unpossessed hope is not the same as a nonexistent hope.

Now they were at the foot of the mountain, almost to the stone gate; the steepness didn't seem to slow them at all. The men strained at the ropes and with a rolling clap of thunder the gate was buried. Smiling and patting each other on the back, Behrlak and the others congratulated themselves on successfully dealing the first blow of the battle. The Taevians began to clog the space beyond the gate, looking from where we stood like a swirling pasture of brown and black grasses that thankfully no longer stretched to the horizon.

From somewhere within the many folds of his azure cape, the wizard-king drew a strange rod. First it was short, then it was long; then he put one end to his right eye and announced that the Taevians were beginning to spill over the top of the stone gate, leaving their horses behind.

Trelm, a young page, appeared at the top of the stairs, behind us, carrying a strange-looking apparatus: an odd connection of sticks and leather. King Treston turned and greeted him with a big smile, nodding for him to come and stand with us. He smiled back and hurried to join us. I didn't know what this contraption he carried was, but evidently the king and queen did. The king seemed to stand more tall and proudly when music such as I'd never heard before began to flow from the instrument without the slightest interruption.

The music cut through the morning air, catching the attention of every soldier on the ridge below, bringing heart-felt grins and hurrahs. Queen Masra disappeared below briefly and returned with an unfamiliar banner, tied to a long pole. She stopped a few paces away, evidently waiting for agreement from the king, whose eyes seemed to be filled with joy. He nodded at last and she came to stand by his side again, planting the bottom of the pole firmly in the dust by her feet. A fresh burst of wind flapped the banner loudly to the side, the sight of it causing the men to cheer yet more loudly and heartily than before.

157

The flag bore a white silhouette of a songbird against a background of deep purple with fine gold fringe sewn to its borders; the wings of the bird were spread as if it were rising into flight.

King Treston turned abruptly to the little one, dropping to one knee. "Go to my private chamber," he said to him, "and bring from the large gilded trunk behind the tapestry the bow and quiver that you find within it. Go, and please hurry." I looked over with a question in my eyes and the king nodded and jerked his head toward the little one disappearing down the stairway. I hurried after him.

He was already in the king and queen's private chamber tugging on a trunk larger than himself when I caught up with the little one.

"Let me help you." I rushed to his side.

With a slow gravelly rumble the trunk slid free of the carved recess in the wall. The lid was flung open before I could even reach for it. Frantically, we shoved aside fine robes, bits of jewelry, and golden goblets. Then I froze for a moment before reaching into the trunk slowly, about to lay hands on a sacred object, the personal weapons of Traenon. I'd never actually seen it before. The little one stood on tiptoe and peered inside. It was beautiful glowing gold: a bow as long as I was tall, a quiver of arrows nearly as long, and a sword with the largest deep blue and red jewels set into the handle that I'd ever seen. Our mouths hung open a long moment. The little one snatched the bow and quiver from my trembling hands and fled down the hallway and up the stairs, leaving me behind in his haste.

King Treston quickly took them and put an arrow to the string. Queen Masra had reappeared immediately behind me as I came up the stairs, evidently from the room of alchemy. She took a strange black cylinder and tied it to the arrow with amazing quickness and dexterity, touching a burning candle to it as the king let it fly.

A long trail of white smoke followed the arrow toward the approaching force. A thunderclap and a burst of smoke shook the mountain just ahead of the Taevians closest to us, creating a small avalanche to bury some of the murderers where they stood.

The little one's eyes flew back and forth between the lingering smoke and the stern gaze of the king. He'd evidently never seen such a thing before, though actually, neither had I.

"There are only three more," the queen cautioned.

"Three more what? What was that thing?" the little one exclaimed.

The king threw a quick smile toward him and drew out another arrow from the quiver. The Taevians were getting close. The other guards began to fill the air with arrows. Most found a mark, but the Taevians were almost to the fortress. I began firing my arrows too.

King Treston fired another thunder-arrow into the almost solid mass of Taevian warriors filling the narrow valley between the fortress and the plain, then another. Nearly all of them had dismounted by now and were in the rocky canyon leading up to the mountain. They were beginning to climb the rocky ledges to the ridge where my friends stood their ground. The Taevians swarmed over the mountain's face like a myriad of insects. Prodono drew his sword and cut down the first to reach them. Nartok formed a chain with Ehrgsos and Ahdrynne to swing out over the ledge, kicking the faces of the invaders away from the rock, sending them tumbling onto the heads of those behind and below. One managed to gain a solid footing on the ridge and was immediately engaged by Velarso, to the villain's quick disadvantage and death.

The wizard-king now laid aside the bow and from within a fold of his clothing drew out a crystal, round and slightly larger than his fist. The outside seemed clear, but the inner depths were like thick black smoke. Balancing the spherical shape between two fingers and the thumb of his right hand, he lifted it high over his head into the bright sunlight. Suddenly a brilliant beam shot from it to rest momentarily on a Taevian marauder. He burst into flames. Those around him nearly shook with fear at the sight, but were swept into the battle by the thousands still pressing forward behind them.

"If only this thing had a wider focus," King Treston muttered, turning the crystal's narrow beam to another enemy soldier, then another, and another.

159

Trelm played his instrument louder, determined to drown out the noises of battle. The wind seemed to blow more fiercely, keeping the flag spread wide and snapping as if alive. Everything seemed to be happening so fast, there was no time to even think. Taevian warriors were pouring over the ridge profusely now, striking my friends from all sides as they went. Nartok was holding two at bay with desperately quick swordsmanship. Blood began running down Velarso's arms from glancing blows.

As the crystal disappeared into a pocket of his robe again, the king's hands closed on the bow once more. "Masra," he shouted. "Now."

His last arrow pressed to the bow string, she tied on the final black cylinder and touched the candle to it. With a vicious hiss the thunder-arrow sliced into the lake's murky depths.

"No!" the little one cried, probably thinking the shot had gone amiss. I couldn't believe the king would do anything so unintentional, but I certainly didn't understand either.

Then with a deep muffled thunder, the wall collapsed. I stared in awe as a deluge rumbled down the mountain, annihilating everything in its path. Boulders bigger than houses were swept from their resting places, pounding the wicked army caught in the flood's path. Those in hand-to-hand combat with my friends, distracted by the sudden trembling of the rock beneath their feet were easily knocked into the torrent's foaming grasp and swept to their graves as well. It all happened so fast. We'd waited for hours. Then it all happened so fast. In moments that seemed to last eternally, it was over.

I glanced at Trelm, still holding his now-silent instrument, his mouth hanging open in awe. The lake was gone. Only a small trickle of water remained where it used to be. Our friends who were yet alive stared at the profusion of bodies and rocks and small trees, stripped and strewn about. The water spilled out onto the plain, finally dispersing with apparent harmlessness.

We hurried to our friends, bandaging wounds as quickly as we could. Nartok was bleeding heavily from a deep cut in his side. Behrlak had many minor cuts, but was too busy tending to his comrades to notice. The little one scurried about crying for

Velarso. Tyren laid a small piece of cloth over someone's face and he ran to see. It was Ahdrynne, our champion swimmer and fisherman. I went to stand next to the little one for a moment and stared at Ahdrynne's youthful face also. A tear ran down the little one's cheek and he bent to wipe a red trickle from the parted friend's lightly tanned cheek. Tyren's sad eyes met mine as he slowly returned the cloth covering our friend's face.

I heard the litte one gasp and turned. Ehrgsos's teeth ground their way into a bow shaft as the limb where his left hand had been was wrapped in strip after strip of white cloth. The little one was almost sobbing now, but I needed to help the others too. As he wheeled around still calling his best friend's name, Velarso appeared from behind a bit of rubble, grabbed his shoulder and caught the little body against his broad chest in bandage-wrapped arms.

I glanced around quickly and was surprised to see that everything was actually already under control. Not knowing how badly Velarso's arms were wounded, I hurried over. He nodded and tipped his head for me to follow as he scooped the little one from the ground and headed back towards the inside of the fortress.

The walls of the lower chambers were still damp from the recently departed water. Finding a reasonably dry place to sit, the three of us briefly hid from the horrors outside. The quietness itself was comforting.

"You've lived among those who've made what you've just seen into their way of life, yet you've never seen them at work?" Velarso said to the little one at last. He winced a little and readjusted his position to take as much pressure as possible off of his arms.

Sniffling a bit and wiping his face, the little one shook his head.

"It's a difficult thing to witness the evil that can be done, one person to another," Velarso said, nodding. "None want to believe that they're capable of the atrocities you've seen today, when the frightening truth is that any of us could do as bad."

The little one tipped his head, perhaps as confused by Velarso's words as I was. He glanced at me when I placed my hands, one on his shoulder and one on the little one's back.

"Rest, my little friend," the wounded warrior said, looking at me again. "But always remember today. It's become a part of who you are, a part of who we all are."

CHAPTER 25

My Continuing Memories: Sifting the Ashes

As the orange glow faded above the plains to the west, the sun sinking slowly from view, we gathered for an evening meal in the lower great hall of the fortress. It wasn't quite the room full of strong and eager soldiers I'd seen the night before. The faces looking back at me were tired and lined with pain. Seventeen of our comrades were to be buried in the morning, assuming of course that those who'd been injured all survived the night.

I looked around at the battered and broken bodies. The king and queen came in, also without saying a word, their faces also lined with a mixture of victory and sadness that mirrored that of the men seated around the large table. The food was served but the room remained relatively silent. No one seemed especially hungry.

"Today has both cost and gained us a great deal," Treston said softly. "And in the morning we'll bury our dead and finish grieving the loss of their company." He looked up to meet the eyes of everyone else in the room. "For tonight, let's give thanks for the lives that remain, the warmth of friendship, and the hope of a better tomorrow."

As if on cue, eyes were closed and faces tipped toward the floor for a long quiet moment. I glanced around, unsure of what was happening. Then heads came up and hands began somberly serving up the bread and meat set before us. The meal passed quietly, not a single word being spoken; each man physically present but seeking mental solitude.

I tried to come to terms with the day's events within myself as I ate, but it all seemed so overwhelming. Then we dispersed for the night, to rest and to heal.

I climbed the stairs to the summit, my feet moving as if made of lead. It was a remarkably clear night with the usual flood of stars across the deep velvet heavens above. The air was peacefully still. Looking down toward the battlefield, the moon showed a few stones moved back, possibly to begin reconstruction of the wall, which would restore the lake.

"You are unhappy, my little friend."

I whirled about, startled.

"Which is perhaps one of the most inane things to say, I suppose," King Treston added, "since we're all saddened by the cost of today's victory."

"In my mind," I responded, "I agree with the need for the battle we fought and the victory we achieved today, but I still find myself asking why."

"Are you concerned with the fate of our departed friends?" the king asked.

I turned my eyes to the stars above again. "Somehow I sense they're still alive somewhere, which doesn't make sense to me, but that I won't be able to see them again for a very long time." I turned to the king and added, "I have a growing number of friendships, it seems, of which that's true for other reasons."

He nodded. "You understand life as a journey on a vast ocean and seasons of friendship as time spent in some seaport or another?"

"I suppose that's as fair an analogy as any," I replied with a sigh. "I've heard it said that nothing lasts forever, but there is no ring of truth in that for me."

"And yet you hesitate as you say that," King Treston said.

"Yes." I sighed. "I hesitate. I've seen times of life and times of friendship come and go like the seasons of the year. Often I wish I could hold tightly enough to a person or a place to possess it always, but that's not the way of living things." Our eyes met a moment--his were patient and quiet, as if knowing what I was about to say. "To force a friendship to last longer than it's appointed for it to last, to refuse to move to a new place when the purpose of the old one's been completed, to reject a new way of seeing and understanding when the world changes and the old way no longer answers the needs I experience. These are as wrong as trees shedding their leaves in spring and flowers beginning to bloom in autumn."

164

"Both encourage death rather than life." He nodded again. "So what are you feeling now?"

"I feel something calling me away," I whispered, staring into the dark and distant horizons of my future.

"Then you must go," the king agreed. "You should take someone with you, perhaps?"

"If I do," I said, "in some way that I don't understand, I'll still be travelling alone. But not because there's any lack of love in my heart for my friends, or vice versa," I added quickly.

"It's okay," he said. "I understand."

I tipped my head quizzically.

"Each is given life for good and specific reasons," Treston explained, "but our lives share more connections than causes. It isn't one life that we share together, but each with his own life, to be governed jointly by the choices we make and the environment we're given. In the world around us, both good and bad things pass by, sometimes very close to us and sometimes farther away. Nevertheless, it's the destiny and purpose of our own life that must continue to guide us."

"And that," I concluded for him, "isn't the easiest thing to discover."

The king smiled and nodded.

"I often suspect that someone great and powerful and wise is watching over me, caring for me, yet always invisible to me. Sometimes I'm allowed to see just a little bit of what my life is all about, but mostly it's hidden from me for reasons I've never been able to grasp." I jerked around to face the king again, as if waking from a sort of dream. "So what will you do now? Where will you go?"

King Treston straightened up, taking a deep breath. "I sense that my distant cousin, King Wolten, the king of Taevius, is still alive, though this time without an army." He paused. "I must go to him to see if we may establish forgiveness and thus peace between the warring peoples of Nypothnia. It's about time, I think, for genuine goodness to again bless the land, that all may live in health, in harmony, and in a truer happiness than we have known."

"Can a defeated king truly forgive?" I asked.

165

"I don't know," he replied, "I don't know whether anyone's ever tried. Perhaps I need his forgiveness as much as he needs mine."

There was a faraway look in the king's eyes; it reminded me of how I must have looked many times during the past few years. I turned to gaze at the night sky one more time. It was time, I decided, for the king to become a traveller and for the traveller to go home.

What is home? Is it something we make or something we're given? Is it a place or a feeling or perhaps a way to be? Maybe it's a situation where we finally know that we belong, just because we are who we are and we know that it's good to be who and what we are.

Maybe it's something that allows us to sleep well at night and smile when we get up in the morning. Perhaps home is where we can treasure our dreams and give them wings, one day at a time. Perhaps it fills our heart with gratitude and peace, a still place of strength stronger than any surrounding turbulence. Perhaps it's simply a place where we can know what it is to be truly alive in the most subtle of ways.

Perhaps it's like a flower which may be planted and cultivated nearly anywhere, which is easily plucked and cut so that it may die while the root sends up another blossom. Pluck as many flowers as you want. Still there will be flowers on the earth, fragile and beautiful, sometimes short-lived but always enduring. I wanted to go home.

CHAPTER 26

Velarso's Chapter

I watched as my little friend knelt beside a particular gravestone. It was Nartok. He'd lost too much blood and died in his sleep during the night. A tear rolled down his face to water the tiny mountain flower planted in the dusty mound. The memory of Nartok's boyish laugh and quick smile made me smile.

Rising to his feet, he quickly scanned the eighteen mountaintop graves once more, pausing at one toward the other end of the row.

I nodded to the little traveller, understanding at once. "Ahdrynne's impish grin and brash willingness to help will live on in us," I told him. "I can never be the same for having known such a friend."

He stood where he was and looked toward the small caravan below, heading out onto the plain. "Oh, Velarso, I do hope King Treston is successful in his quest for peace." He turned to me. "Why did the crystals we were given not preserve the lives of our friends?"

"In the midst of battle," I faltered, trying to think of a wise answer, "we're often too distracted to remember all of the advantages we possess. If only we'd remembered, if only, if only..." I sighed. "If only we could more easily accept that things have turned out as they have and can't be undone. Nevertheless, it's right and good for us to grieve."

"Do you think we'll ever be here again?" he asked.

"In this physical place, no. In this moment of loss and decision and transition, probably many times." I said, casting my gaze across the row of graves one more time. "There are many places longing to receive our footprints, our handprints." I looked into the little one's eyes. "Our lifeprints."

He nodded silently, surveying the summit one last time.

"I have our provisions," I said, "a couple of swords, and your brown cloak in the pack strapped to my back--whenever you're ready to go."

He nodded again, stepping closer to me but still looking around at the majestic peaks to the east and the vast plain to the west where our friends were fading into the distance.

He turned to me again, regarding my bandaged arms and the long, deep blue cape draped over both my shoulders and the pack I wore. He wore a tunic of pale blue and a short cape of purple. I smiled a little, noticing that he actually looked quite handsome for the first time since I'd known the little one.

With a boyish laugh and an impish grin, he leapt into my arms. His short arms couldn't manage too much of a hug so I held onto him instead, laughed and spun around playfully.

"Okay?" I said and looked into his eyes again.

"Okay," he replied and returned the gentle stare.

"Then concentrate," I said, closing my eyes. "Picture everything just as it is there, the busy road to Avinngra, a city half in ruins but still the social and economic center of Nypothnia." There was a sudden flash of light that penetrated my eyelids and the sound of a strong wind, so loud that all other sounds were swept away. A sudden weightlessness almost threw me off-balance and I felt the little one grip my hands more tightly. Then I heard other voices, the lowing of cattle, and the calls of sheep and goats and chickens. "We're here," I said. "You can open your eyes." His grip on my fingers relaxed and I knelt and put an arm across his shoulders.

"It worked," he shouted, "and they're rebuilding Avinngra!"

There it was, the road to the main gate now filled with farmers coming to barter what they had for what they needed, and the surrounding hills and forests just as I remembered.

"It's amazing," he whispered to me, as we drew closer to the main gates. "I was told that this city lay in ruins, but look. It's being rebuilt."

"Destruction is rarely successful in being as complete and permanent as it nearly always claims to be," I said, grinning. "It looks like the population here is growing rapidly too."

"I had a good friend who lived in a town near here once, Brenwill, the carpenter," my little friend said, "but he was killed during a Taevian raid. There are so many things I wish I'd told him, things I wish I'd been brave enough to say to him, but I wasn't ready and the chance slipped away too quickly."

I stopped, dropping to one knee beside him when we were just inside the gate. "But you have this day and the chance to live it without regrets. Do all the good you can while you have opportunity because opportunities won't always be there."

"I couldn't have said it better myself," the little one answered. "Where is that music coming from?" He tipped his head to catch the faint melody on the breeze.

"This way, I believe," I said, leading toward the left, onto a wider street that finally emptied into a large courtyard, a sort of public market.

There, surrounded by a rapt crowd, stood a troubadour.

"Jonathon Ellick," the little one shouted, starting to run.

"Yo, Taevian," called a booming voice. I grabbed my little friend's shoulder with one hand and the hilt of my sword with the other.

The marketplace was instantly silent as heads whirled in our direction. Then a poor old hag with a few teeth missing spied the little one and started to scream.

Taking a deep breath and straightening up, he forced a definite and polite smile in her direction. The scream died in her throat. She tipped her head, confused. I turned again, still seeking the source of the booming voice and discovered the giant form of Gairen, the archer. The little one grinned and I burst into a joyous laugh as the giant scooped our tiny friend from the ground onto his massive shoulders, high above the crowd around us. I saw the little one look toward the troubadour again, but his smile faded when this Jonathon Ellick as he'd called him barely even responded. I felt disappointed too, somehow.

"So speak to me, my little friend," Gairen said to the little man on his shoulders, interrupting my disappointed thoughts. "Where've you been and what've you been up to?"

"Oh, there's so much to tell," I interrupted, grinning.

169

The people around us stood transfixed by the sight of such a giant man with such a small friend. "Tell us," I heard someone shout. "Tell us the tales."

The little one glanced toward Jonathon again, but the troubadour was silent.

"But you," a young girl called out, "the strange little one. Who are you?"

He looked down toward me, his face almost a question, and I answered with my biggest, most sincere smile. Then the little traveller responded with eyes deep with understanding and a grin all his own, "I am myself. I am myself!"

About The Author

Denver NeVaar grew up in a small farming community in Wisconsin and has been writing creatively since before his tenth birthday. Obviously creative and artistically gifted since even before his first year of formal schooling, his life experience has been a thorough teacher in what it is to be an anomaly and to face the challenges of making one's own uniqueness into something very good. <u>Troll Steps</u> was begun while in college and finished five years later while he and his life-partner were living high in the mountains of Colorado. In being a minister with a passion for spirituality, personal growth, and deep understanding of life itself, he brings to the craft of literature a quality that can reach to the depths of the human soul. Through the process of his own self-discovery, Denver learned what it is to look into the mirror and see nothing and to look again and see a more beautiful person than anyone thought was there. The experience of such a process of personal growth is most definitely at the heart of the journey of <u>Troll Steps</u>--a journey that will continue for ages to come.